Love is
a time of enchantment:
in it all days are fair and all fields
green. Youth is blest by it,
old age made benign:
the eyes of love see
roses blooming in December,
and sunshine through rain. Verily
is the time of true-love
a time of enchantment — and
Oh! how eager is woman
to be bewitched!

NURSE IN THE VALLEY

Sally Wakefield SRN wondered if she'd done the right thing to leave the wards of dear old 'Kit's' for the big, noisy Works in a little Welsh valley. Some of her colløeagues resented her not being Welsh; certainly Richard Llewellyn did. She was grateful for the attention of Huw Thomas, her 'doctor on call'. Before she finally won through, Sally experienced many traumatic moments and much heart-searching.

Books by Grace Goodwin
in the Ulverscroft Large Print Series:

A DREAM FOR TOMORROW
LYDIA'S DAUGHTER

GRACE GOODWIN

NURSE IN THE VALLEY

Complete and Unabridged

ULVERSCROFT
Leicester

First published in Great Britain in 1987 by
Robert Hale Limited
London

First Large Print Edition
published June 1992
by arrangement with
Robert Hale Limited
London

British Library CIP Data

Goodwin, Grace
  Nurse in the valley.—Large print ed.—
  Ulverscroft large print series: romance
  I. Title
  823.914 [F]

  ISBN 0–7089–2661–4

Published by
F. A. Thorpe (Publishing) Ltd.
Anstey, Leicestershire
Set by Words & Graphics Ltd.
Anstey, Leicestershire
Printed and bound in Great Britain by
T. J. Press (Padstow) Ltd., Padstow, Cornwall

1

SALLY — Sarah Elizabeth Wakefield, SRN — Ward Sister of St Christine's — moistened her dry top lip nervously, her slim, capable hands folded tightly in her lap. Calmly, she faced the semicircle on the opposite side of the old-fashioned office.

She had answered all the questions the managing director had put to her with confidence, secure in the knowledge that her references were impeccable, her qualifications of the highest. Apart from the manager seated behind the large, leather-topped desk, there was also the Chief Security Officer, the young nurse who would be her assistant, and the Personnel Officer.

It was the latter whose demeanour had her puzzled. Ever since the interview for the post of Sister-in-Charge had begun, she had felt his animosity. Tall and dark, his face was stern and cold, his grey eyes full of a dislike that made Sally wonder why he resented her so?

"It is usual for our chief nurse to also hold an Occupational Health certificate." Sally brought her attention back to the stout man behind the desk. "However," he went on, "your wide experience is quite good enough, Sister."

Smiling, obviously wanting to end the interview, he looked round at the others for their approval. The PO at the window looking over the busy forecourt below, swung round, and once more his eyes glanced coldly across at Sally.

"One thing, Sister Wakefield, rather intrigues me," he said. "Why are you leaving St Christine's? Why leave the big city of Birmingham to come here — to a little valley town in South Wales?"

Sally caught her breath, swallowing hard before she answered quietly:

"I have my reasons, Mr Llewellyn. Private reasons which will not affect my working here! I — I wanted a change from hospital wards, and this job appealed to me. It's different — a new challenge," she ended, her hazel eyes steady as she faced this man whose dislike she could feel across the room.

2

Why? she wondered. Had he hoped to see a Welsh girl in this post; was that the reason for his obvious animosity?

Shrugging his broad shoulders, he gave the managing director his assenting nod — grudgingly so nevertheless!

"Very well, Sister," the boss rose, holding out his hand, "the position's yours. When can you start?"

"Thank you, sir." Sally took his hand. "A month from tomorrow?"

"Very well." He passed on to the next pile of papers needing his attention. "Mr Llewellyn and — er — Nurse Evans will show you round. Goodbye for now."

With a quiet farewell, Sally picked up her bag and followed the others out of the office. Once outside, the PO turned abruptly.

"Megan here will show you round your working areas, Sister. I'll see you in a month's time. Goodbye for now."

Despite its attractive Welsh lilt, his voice was cold and his manner showed his deep antipathy. Bewildered and angry at his attitude, Sally gave him a curt "Goodbye," and followed the young nurse. Not that *her* manner was very

3

friendly either! As she followed the sturdy figure, Sally wondered if she was making a mistake? Or perhaps she was seeing difficulties where there weren't any? Given time, she would get used to these people — get to understand their ways.

"This is our Surgery." Megan pushed open the heavy door, her defensive attitude defying any criticism. Sally cast a professional eye quickly round, noting the drugs cupboard, the high couch, the desk and equipment.

Just in time, she stopped herself from passing an exploratory fingertip from habit over the ridges for dust, and she could see lots of things *she* would want improving!

"Three cubicles by there, and a little rest room next to Sister's office. All very nice, isn't it?"

Megan's round Welsh face wore a look of proprietorial pride, and Sally nodded with a smile.

"The records are kept here, Sister. You will have the key. Doctor Thomas uses your office for his twice weekly surgeries too. Idris Williams — he's the night shift first-aider — he has a little place nearer the mills for his use. Very good, he is, but bossy with it," Megan finished, and wisely Sally ignored this last remark; time to make up her own mind later!

"Would you like to see round the Works? A good chance, it is . . . "

Sally nodded. "Yes, please. Though I don't want to take you away from your duties."

But Megan was already lifting the phone.

"Dai — Mr Jones, Security, will take you round, Sister."

"Thanks, Megan. I — I hope we're going to work together well — I shall be depending on you a lot at first."Her warm smile lit up her face, and for a moment it was almost beautiful with its fine cheek bones and clear skin. Her dark-lashed eyes held something very appealing in them right then as she turned to the young assistant.

But Megan shrugged, her lips set with an uncompromising tightness.

"Seem funny, it will, working with an English sister . . . "

So that was it! Sally gave a soft sigh

and turned as the Security Officer came in. Middle-aged, David Jones was a well set-up man with a warm, welcoming smile. His navy uniform suit was neat, his white collar spotless, his grey hair well-trimmed and his manner friendly.

"Come on then, Sister, and I'll show you around . . . " And for the next half-hour he took her through huge mills, furnaces, rolling plant and extrusion works. The heat and noise was terrible, and for a moment Sally wondered how she could possibly consider changing her clean, quiet ward for this?

Occasionally, David Jones frowned at the sight of strewn cables, chains and pulleys — all sources of danger.

"They never learn, the boys . . . " he muttered shaking his grey head. Sally's temples were beginning to ache when he asked —

"Fancy a cup of tea, Sister? I'll make us one in my little office."

And soon she was perched on a stool in his little cubby-hole near the huge main gates. From there he could see everything that passed by into the yards. Heavy lorries loaded with bulky metal;

workmen, their faces grimed with grease, all checked here first. As she sipped the strong, hot tea, Sally asked him —

"What exactly do you make here, Mr Jones?"

"Call me Dai, Sister, more friendly it is." His chest swelled importantly. "We make all the components needed for dust extraction plant, see?" At her look of bewilderment, he went on, "Used more and more these days, lass. The new micro-chip works — can't have a speck of dust there, can they? And nuclear works and so on. Very important, we are."

Now she understood what their name meant — Dustrax Components Limited.

"Want to see the offices, Sister, and the canteen? Mostly females there."

Remembering the interested glances from the men, she shook her head.

"No, thanks, Dai. Plenty of time next month." Smiling, she refused another cup of tea and rose to go. The taxi would soon be here to take her back into town and the sooty little railway station.

"What about digs, Sister — you fixed up?"

"No — not till I got the post." Sally

knitted her brows. "I suppose there's a little hotel I could stay at until I got somewhere?"

The Security Officer rubbed his chin thoughtfully, watching Sally's face.

"I'm wondering — I have a young relative — on her own a lot. Too much so, I reckon. She has plenty of room; nice girl she is — clean, too."

A few minutes later Sally had made up her mind to go and see young Mrs Hughes and take a later train. Cordially thanking Dai Jones, she took the slip of paper giving the address and left his little office. Outside the gates, she paused and looked back at the huge, grimy buildings; as unlike a hygienic hospital as they could possibly be! At one of the office windows stood a tall, dark man looking down, and even without clearly seeing his face, Sally knew it was Richard Llewellyn! And a cold chill ran through her veins.

"Your taxi, Miss. To the station, is it?" Sally shook her head.

"Er — no — to this address, please."

She found Caradoc Terrace near to the centre of town. A street of tall, Victorian

8

houses — some badly in need of a coat of paint, others brightly modernized. No. 12 had spotlessly clean curtains Sally noticed as she waited after ringing the bell.

"Mamma, mamma — someone's at the door." There was the sound of a child's shrill voice, and then the door opened.

Myfanwy Hughes was a plump, plain young woman with a faint droop to her lips. Beside her, a shy, dark-eyed little girl looked up at Sally inquisitively. Explaining why she had come, Sally went on —

"Of course, if it's not convenient just now . . . ?"

"No, it's all right. Please come in. Ceri, let the lady by now. My husband's working away, only gets home for short times. I mentioned a while ago to Uncle Dai that perhaps a lady lodger would be a good thing. There's a big room to spare, only it's right up top, see?"

"I wouldn't mind that, Mrs Hughes; I'll be working."

"Come by here then, and I'll show you."

It was a big room, light and airy, across the length of the house, and

Sally could see at once that it had great possibilities.

"I'll put some more bits and pieces in for you, er . . . ?"

"Call me Sally — Sally Wakefield."

"And I'm Myfanwy, and this is my Ceri." The eight-year-old hung her head. "She's shy now, but wait 'til she knows you, Sally, she'll talk you to death." There was a wealth of love in the young mother's voice.

Downstairs again in the warm kitchen, Sally turned and held out her hand.

"I'll take it, Myfanwy. I'll let you know when I'm coming . . . "

The terms were very reasonable, and promising to get in touch, Sally wrote down her telephone number.

"I'll be bringing a few things in my car. Till then, thanks Myfanwy. I'm sure I'll be fine here."

The young woman's face flushed with pleasure, and Sally thought she could be quite pretty if she tried. She pressed a coin into the little girl's hand.

"For sweeties," she whispered. "Bye, Ceri, be seeing you, pet."

By the time Myfanwy had shown her to

the door, Sally felt that she had made one friend down here. Two, if you counted Dai Jones. As for the others . . . ? She shrugged her slim shoulders, and decided to walk the short distance to the station — perhaps get a bite to eat too on the way.

It was getting dark by the time her train departed, and Sally suddenly felt tired and unsure of herself. Was she doing the right thing, she wondered? She'd miss her friends at St Christine's, especially Roz, her room-mate — and what would her parents say?

She turned her face to the spotted window, watching the dark iron structure of the Severn Bridge and the muddy river banks below. What else could she do? She couldn't stay on at St Christine's — not now. She blinked at the sudden sting of tears behind her eyelids, biting her soft lip at the pain of her thoughts. She wished she didn't have to serve a month's notice — God knows it would be difficult.

If only she didn't have to see Philip again . . .

She remembered so clearly her first real meeting with Philip. She had been Ward Sister in charge of Men's Surgical for about six months, and was lucky to be one of the fortunate nurses allowed to share a flat away from the hospital.

It had been somewhere for hungry doctors, nurses and students to drop in, and there was lots of gossip, borrowing and lending, sharing of news. That is until exams came round, and then silence descended like a pall!

Sally and her room-mate, Roz, were helping the latest batch of young doctors to celebrate — or bemoan their exam results when she met Philip Chandon. Really met him, that is, without a group of student doctors trailing behind him. He was a consultant on loan to St Christine's. As so many doctors came and went, Sally knew little about Philip. She'd heard junior nurses giggle, trying to attract the new man's attention, praising his good looks and bedside manner.

Then at the party she'd looked up to find his eyes watching her intently.

"You look charming, Sally, out of uniform, I mean."

Not a very original line, but Sally's heart leapt at the admiration in Philip's eyes, and they spent the rest of the party chatting together, oblivious of the crowd around them.

Philip was ambitious; Sally realized that right from the start; clever, keen to get on, he was well on the way up. He was popular with every one, although strangely enough no-one really knew much about him — unusual in such a close community where everyone knew everything! But somehow Philip had a clever knack of avoiding any too-personal questions, dodging the issue without your being aware that he had done so . . .

"Let me stay the night, Sally, darling. Roz's on duty and you're all alone."

It was getting harder and harder to refuse Philip's pleas. He wanted her, and what Philip Chandon wanted, he usually got! Did her refusals make him all the keener? Heaven knows there were plenty of girls willing to oblige the handsome consultant — Matron's secretary, Mavis, made no secret of the fact! *Her* envy and bitchy pinpricks were causing Sally a lot of irritation.

Now his kisses were making her pulses race; it was so hard to refuse him.

"No, Philip, I'm sorry, but I don't want to get involved in that way, unless we are going to marry. I love you, darling, it's so hard to say No, but . . . "

Looking back, she realized that *she* had been the one to mention marriage, not Philip! Oh, he had said he loved her, wanted her, but had never spoken of their future together.

Seated there in the dusty railway carriage, remembering, Sally's lovely brown eyes filled with tears, her lips tightened with bitterness. Remembering . . .

It was during the summer epidemic, when the hospital had scarcely a bed to spare, that Sally went down with a bad tummy bug that laid her low and tearful, missing Philip. But as he explained, he couldn't risk being infected, too, could he? Apart from carefully worded little messages, she had no contact with him and found herself longing for his loving and kisses.

14

Roz fussed around her all the time, until at last Sally burst out —

"For heaven's sake, Roz, cut out the ministering angel bit, love. It's a tummy bug, nothing worse."

But Roz stood there, unconsciously pleating the edge of the bedcover between her fingers, her usual sunny face anxious-looking. And Sally, gazing up into her friend's face had asked —

"What *is* the matter, Roz?"

Roz swallowed hard, and then rushed on —

"I must tell you, Sally — before you hear from someone else . . . " She paused, reluctant to go on.

"Tell me what?"

"It's Philip," Roz blurted out. "He's — the swine — he's already married, Sally!"

Shock hit Sally like a savage blow.

"Married?"

"Yes, I got it from Matron's secretary, Mavis." Roz paced the room in agitation. "Oh, she just *loved* telling me, didn't she? Apparently, Philip's wife rang up wanting to speak to him urgently. Big-Ears Mavis kept her chatting whilst he was being brought to the phone. Lord knows just what poison she poured into Mrs Philip's ears. You know Mavis is another one who fancies the dishy doctor. But we — I never dreamed he was married, did you, Sally?"

Turning to look at her friend, Roz was shocked by the desperate pallor of her face, as white as the pillows around her.

"I'm so sorry, Sal . . . "

It was the pity of her colleagues that Sally found hardest to bear. She avoided the staff canteen just as Philip was avoiding her; apart from a brief nod as he sped down the corridor past her ward, she hadn't seen him at all. Then after a week of hiding herself away, of tears, Sally's natural sturdy spirit began to lift again. Why should she mourn the loss of a man who belonged to another woman, and who was ready to deceive them both? The grapevine gossip had it that his wife was a very quiet kind of girl who happened to have a bit of money of her own when Philip married her. Poor girl — Sally wondered if Philip had tried to be unfaithful to his wife before?

Thank heavens she hadn't given way to his pleadings and slept with him! He hadn't really loved her; why should she mourn the loss of such a rotter? Determined to ignore the whisperings, she squared her stubborn chin, vowing to put the heartache behind her.

All the same, working at St Christine's suddenly lost its appeal and, after much heart-searching, Sally decided to leave. Finally, it was the Nursing Agency who offered her the chance of the post as Industrial Sister-in-Charge at the works in the little South Wales town.

"A steel works . . . ?" She couldn't keep the doubt out of her voice. The Principal of the Agency fingered the notes on her desk.

"Well, you did say you wanted a complete change. You'll be in charge, with an assistant, and there's a near-by doctor on call for anything serious; comes in twice a week. The salary is very good, too." She looked across her desk at Sally's rather wan face. "Do you good, my dear," she said kindly sensing the inner sadness that caused the unhappy look on the Sister's face.

More briskly she went on, "Anyway, why not go down for the interview, fares and expenses paid? Shall I tell them to expect you, Sister Wakefield?"

It certainly sounded far enough away from St Christine's and utterly different.

"Yes, please," Sally answered collecting all the details she needed. She had made her first decisive step towards forgetting Philip!

Roz and a few of Sally's set were giving her a farewell party, and the small flat was full of young nurses and doctors. White coats, belts and caps were thankfully discarded, many were in stockinged feet; the noise was deafening. Everyone wanted to hear about Sally's new job; tactfully refraining from mentioning Philip's name. Sally knew there was a few who were dying to do so, especially Mavis! Half-way through the evening, there was a sudden unexpected hush, and Sally looked up to see Philip's tall figure standing in the doorway. Her heart jerked and then went on thudding painfully, her face pale. But she was determined not to let him know how deeply his deceit had hurt her.

"Hi, Philip!" she called out gaily. "Glad you could make it. Can I get you a drink?" It was an effort, but Sally was proud of the steadiness of her voice, and her lips twisted wryly as she saw the obvious relief on Philip's face. Had he expected her to make a scene; was his appearance here tonight just his way of facing her again — in public? Where she couldn't make a scene anyway? Bitter gall burned the back of her throat.

"Thanks, Sally. Thought I'd just drop in and — er — wish you all the best for the new job."

He didn't stay long, and Sally's friends threw themselves into making the party even more of a success. She knew they meant well, but somehow she felt sick.

Her last day was a wrench; after all she had spent all her nursing days at St Christine's, but twenty-five was too young to get into a rut anyway . . .

Her little car was crammed full inside and the roof rack bulged with her belongings in spite of the fact that she had left a lot of things at home. Her bewildered parents had tactfully refrained from asking questions and Sally was grateful.

She sighed softly and relaxed to take in the lovely Wye Valley scenery. Then at last she passed the busy little dock, the cranes towering over muddy banks where the River Usk and River Severn met. Turning the car towards No. 12 Caradoc Terrace, Sally received a warm welcome from Myfanwy Hughes and little Ceri.

As they all toiled up the steep flight of stairs, her landlady gasped —

"I do hope you'll be all right here, Sally?" and she pushed open the door with her foot.

"I'm sure . . . oh, it looks lovely!" Sally's cry of pleasure made Myfanwy's face light up. She had worked hard, and the long, low-ceilinged room looked fresh and cosy. The curtains and covers were of Laura Ashley cotton; a table and easy chair stood beneath the dormer window, and Sally noticed she had her own electric kettle.

"Thank you very much, Myfanwy, I'll be fine here."

"Where shall I put these?" Young Ceri was struggling with a heap of small packages, her eyes bright with excitement.

"You look a bit warm, pet," Sally's professional eye took in the little girl's flushed face.

"Yes, she seems to have a bit of a temperature. It's the excitement, I shouldn't wonder."

Later as they sat drinking a welcome cup of tea in the homely kitchen, Sally asked —

"And what does your husband say about your lodger, Myfanwy?"

A shadow passed over Myfanwy's smooth round face, and her fingers curled tightly around her cup.

"I don't know; I haven't heard, see? He's not much of a letter writer, my man," and something in her voice made Sally's heart ache.

"Well, you won't be quite so alone now, will you, love?"

The next morning, Ceri's temperature was higher; her face flushed, her eyes pink and watery. She felt very sorry for herself indeed when Sally went in to see her.

"What a pretty room, Ceri — and so many lovely dolls . . . " Diverting the child's attention, she was able to make a quick examination. Then tucking the blanket closer, she crossed over and drew the dainty frilled curtains nearer together.

Downstairs, she saw that Myfanwy's face was worriedly anxious as she waited to hear the worst!

"Don't worry, pet, it's only German measles. If I were you, I'd get all her little girl friends bundled in that bed with her! German measles can be bad for young expectant mums — better if all females had it as children." Sally paused. "By the way, you're not . . . ?"

"Pregnant — no! Fat chance," Myfanwy muttered bitterly. "I'll ring the doctor and keep her in bed, shall I? What a rotten start to your stay here, Sally," she added worriedly.

"If there's nothing worse facing me at the Works, love, I won't grumble! Bye now, see you tonight — and don't worry . . . "

2

THE rugged mountains which surrounded the town were still shrouded in mist when Sally turned her car in the Works' gates. The Security Officer was dealing with the driver of an articulated lorry full of scrap metal. There seemed to be some sort of an argument going on, and Dai Jones' face was troubled when he came across to speak to her.

"Morning, Sister, you're nice and early. Have you settled in at young Myfanwy's, then?"

"Good morning, Mr Jones. Yes, I'm fine there; thanks for recommending her to me." She wondered why he was scowling after the departing lorry, then realized it was none of her business! Still, she liked this open-faced man — and then, as if reading her mind, he muttered —

"Something wrong there, I reckon." He tugged at his ear and then smiled down at Sally. "That's your parking place over there, Sister. Good luck on your first day . . . "

"Thanks — be seeing you."

She had changed into her white uniform dress, perched the little cap on her chestnut-coloured hair and was going through the cupboards when Megan Evans came in. Surprised, the young girl looked at her watch.

"It's all right, Megan, I'm early. What time's sick parade?" She flipped open the big casebook on the desk.

"About ten o'clock, Sister. Doctor Thomas will be here after his own surgery — about eleven o'clock usually."

"Oh good — plenty of time to do these cupboards out then before surgery." Sally began to roll up her sleeves, then tied a plastic apron round her slim waist.

"I cleaned out the cupboards last week." Megan's face was set and stubborn-looking.

"I just love scrubbing out cupboards, Megan, takes me back to my probationer days. Besides, I'd like these bottles re-labelled like this . . . " Sally began to show the young nurse how *she* wanted things done. Whether Megan liked it or not, everything would be according to Sister Sarah Wakefield from now on!

Grudgingly, reluctantly, Megan started to work.

"I usually have a coffee first," she grumbled.

"Didn't you have any breakfast?"

Megan's face flushed. "No — got up too late."

Sally raised an eyebrow in the young nurse's direction — it spoke volumes!

"We might have time for coffee before sick roll . . . "

Sally hated the sullen atmosphere, but she intended to start as she meant to go on, whether Megan liked it or not! Besides the cupboards were dirty in the corners; the various bottles and containers were sticky, the labels hardly decipherable. Happily she wiped the surfaces with an antiseptic and the place began to look and smell better. Later she would give the whole Medical Unit a good clean for, probably used to the grime of coal mines and steel works, their standard of cleanliness was not good enough for Sally.

"The cleaners do that work, Sister. You are here for a different job!" She spun round at the sound of the harsh voice.

Richard Llewellyn stood in the doorway, his stern face showing his disapproval. Peeling off her rubber gloves, Sally faced him, chin squared, her lips firm.

"Did I hear you knock, Mr Llewellyn?" she asked coldly.

"Knock? Of course not! I came by to see if you'd turned up. I never knock around here."

"Perhaps not, but from now on, *everyone* knocks and waits before entering this Medical Unit. Privacy is a privilege necessary for sick people — and sister-in-charge! I'll put a notice on the door."

Richard Llewellyn's face flushed a dull, angry red as he obviously held back his wrath.

"Did you hear the chap outside then? He's bleeding all over the place! I suggest you leave the spring cleaning to the cleaners and attend to your own job!"

How dare he speak to her like that — the great Welsh git! Sally's temper almost boiled over, and only the sight of

Megan's watchful face made her control it. She began to scrub her hands.

"Send him in, Mr Llewellyn — thank you." Her tone was like ice — two could play at being nasty!

A cheerfully smiling workman came through holding his finger aloft.

"I win the bet, Sister. 'Twas to see who got in to meet you the first. Could've done without this though," he added ruefully.

'This' was a piece of wire which was piercing his finger. Quickly, efficiently, Sally cleansed the wound and with one swift tug of her surgical pliers had the offending wire out and the finger dressed.

"Now — trousers down, Mr . . . " she commanded briskly.

"Me trousers?" The shock on his face was laughable.

"Yes, you need an anti-tetanus jab after that. Sorry."

His face paled visibly.

"The needle," he gasped, "I hate the needle . . . " and he was puzzled when Sally gave an attractive little chuckle of laughter, not seeing the joke until she explained —

"I've just taken a piece of wire out that's worse than any needle!"

As she talked to him, she gently gave him the necessary injection.

"Wait in the other room for a while to see if you've taken . . . "

The waiting-room was now filling, and during the session Sally was surprised to notice how many men were complaining of tummy ache! After the fourth examination, she began to wonder — were they trying to pull a fast one on her, wanting to see what the new sister was like?

Later, as she went back to check her anti-tetanus injection result, the friendly chap whispered —

"You have to make out a form, see, pet."

"A form?"

"Yes, all the accidents have forms. Them — over there . . . "

Crossing the surgery, she discovered the pad of forms in triplicate. Apparently she kept one; one went to the Safety Officer, who did a check on any equipment that had caused the accident, and the final slip went to the Personnel Officer for his records.

"Do that every time, you do, Sister."

"Thanks for telling me. I've a lot to learn today." She was annoyed that her assistant had not seen fit to inform her of this important procedure.

There was a clatter of boots as two hefty men, supporting another between them, hustled through the door.

"Fainted, he did, Sister. Must have been them furnaces — terrible hot, like."

"Put him down here, please." She indicated the high couch.

Quickly she loosened the man's collar. He was recovering, but still looked dazed and shaken. She took his pulse and temperature, creasing her forehead as she did so.

"I want you to, stay here quietly for a while and then see the doctor."

There was an anxious look in the man's eyes, and beneath the dirt on his face, he was pale and drawn.

"Won't do any harm to get Doctor Thomas to check, will it? Megan will bring you a cup of tea soon."

The next man was a new employee reporting to her for his medical checks — blood, urine, etc. Once more she had to make out the necessary forms for several different departments; this time for the Pension Fund too.

"Lot of writing, isn't there, Sister?" She looked up into Megan's face and its smug, satisfied look angered her.

"It would have helped if I had been told about all these various forms. But you're not being too helpful, are you, Megan?"

The younger girl's face flushed and she shrugged.

"More interested in cleaning out cupboards, you were, Sister." Before she could answer, the door opened and a pleasant-faced man breezed in.

"Sister Wakefield? I'm Huw Thomas." He shook hands cordially, and Sally liked the feel of his firm handclasp, was charmed by the warmth of his greeting and the admiration on his round, smooth-skinned face.

He was rather younger than she'd expected — about forty-five, of average height like all these local Welshmen (with the exception of the towering Richard Llewellyn!). The doctor was plumper too, but right then his friendliness was just what she needed.

"A cup of coffee, please, Megan, before I begin. Been up the Valley all night with a first baby delivery."

Shedding his coat, he sprawled opposite Sally, his twinkling brown eyes watching her face.

"Finding it a bit strange, are you Sister, after the wards?" Without giving her time to answer, he went on, "Never mind, you'll soon settle down. Fine bunch of lads we have here."

Sally took a cup of coffee from Megan, saying, "Give our fainting chap a cup of sweet tea, will you, please?"

They sat, sipping the welcome brew, looking at each other, both liking what they saw!

"Must say you're a great improvement, Sister. Not that Nurse wasn't good at her job, but . . . " he glanced mischievously round, "but oh, she was so plain. Now you," he beamed happily. "We'll have surgery full to brimming every day, I reckon."

Sally coloured at his blatant admiration. If only the Personnel Officer was a little more like the friendly doctor!

31

"Now — what have you for me today?" he asked briskly. Sally consulted her list.

"New man to OK, a sprain to check ready for back to work. I'm a bit anxious about all these with stomach pains. Could be genuine — or a put-on." She answered his grin with one of her own. "Also I've a chap out there, fainted at work, but I think he could be an epileptic."

He gave her a sharp glance, and for a second Sally wondered if she could be wrong.

"An epileptic? No — never! We never employ even the mildest *petit mal* suspect in the Works, far too dangerous."

But she sat firm and Huw Thomas frowned.

"Let's see him. My God, how did he get through?"

Megan brought the man in, and once more Sally was struck by his downcast manner; he was obviously worried about something! With a soothing lilt to his voice, his manner kind and gentle, the doctor gradually had the man more relaxed. Carefully he examined and questioned him, and as he did, Sally could see that he was beginning to agree with her diagnosis.

"Well, Ted boyo, we'll make a few tests, eh? Can't have you flopping out like a big wench, can we?"

Mumbling, the man tucked his shirt into his trousers, and when he'd gone the doctor looked up at Sally.

"Nice work, Sister, I believe you're right. I'll arrange for some tests at the local hospital. Poor devil, tried to keep it quiet, but he's a danger to himself and his workmates."

They worked well together through the surgery session and when he was getting ready to leave, Huw Thomas patted her shoulder.

"A big improvement, you are, *cariad*," and the look in his sparkling eyes made her flush with pleasure. "Cheer the chaps up more than any medicine."

"Will it be all right, Doctor, if I do a few checks in the canteen? Could be a touch of food poisoning causing the stomach pains — they all ate in the canteen yesterday, I understand."

Huw Thomas pursed his lips.

"The canteen! You may be right there

again, Sister, but I'd rather you tackle the formidable Gwyneth Harris than me!"

"That bad, is she?"

"Not with the men, but you — oh, she'll hate you, Sister dear. You're far too young and pretty. Must go — good luck. Take it easy at first, eh?"

She had a nasty gash to suture, a suspected concussion to send home, and two pairs of eyes to clear of steel splinters before lunch.

"What about the lunch-time rota, Megan?"

"We used to take it turn-about, one early, one later."

"That's fine," Sally replied cheerfully. "Draw up a list and I'll give you first choice."

There was no thaw in the young nurse's attitude, and as she began checking the surgery and waiting-room, Sally sighed, wondering how long she would be able to work with Megan Evans without losing her temper.

"I'll go early this week then, Sister."

"Fine. And I'll start making out a new list of requisitions, we're low on a lot of things. When you come back, go through it and see if you need to add to it, will you, please?"

With a curt nod, Megan picked up her handbag and went for her lunch. She must have contacted the PO on her way, for as Sally began her list, there was a loud knocking on the door and she rose to admit a stern-faced Richard Llewellyn. She almost felt like slamming the door in his face, however, she returned to her little desk and faced him calmly.

"Yes . . . ?"

"This chap you've had in this morning — fainted. You say he's an epileptic?"

"We're not sure; we're having some further tests made," she replied.

"Well, you're wrong! We don't employ epileptics here. Not on the shop floor, that is. Too damn dangerous." Sally could tell he was worried — someone had slipped up and he knew it!

"I agree, Mr Llewellyn. Shall we wait for the test results before we blow our top?"

Her calm manner, her refusal to be intimidated annoyed him, but Sally thought she saw a flash of respect in his dark eyes as he told her —

"Meanwhile, I'll move the chap to another job. He won't like that so you'd better be right, Sister."

Sally gave him a sweet smile. "I usually am," she replied softly. He gave a snort of derision and slammed out, leaving Sally still puzzled by his attitude. Why did he resent her so . . . ?

The canteen was still full and steamy with the clatter of chairs, of pots and pans and the loud chatter of men used to talking above the din of machinery, and the noise hit Sally deafeningly as she passed through the swing doors. There was a sudden hush at the tables nearest the doors, and her colour rose as the men paused in their eating to stare openly at the new sister.

There were one or two long, low whistles, a buzz of comments, and it took all her courage to outstare the blatant glances of the men nearby. Shoulders squared, a smile round her soft lips, she made her way to the end of the counter and picked up a tray. Plenty of solid stuff, chips and other popular choices. You could have heard a pin drop as she moved along the counter; the girls serving the food watching her every move. knowing what heavy stodge could do to her figure now that she wasn't dashing about her ward, she decided on a cheese salad and wholemeal roll, with fruit yoghourt to follow.

As she got to the cash till, she heard a loud sniff of scorn and looked up into the face of a tall, peroxide blonde looking down at her tray with a grimace of disapproval. No need to ask who this was! Well, thought Sally, here we go . . .

"Hello, are you the manageress? I'm Sister Wakefield — new here today."

"Mrs Gwyneth Harris, that's me. You'll not keep your strength up on that," the woman nodded her brassy head at Sally's tray.

"Have to watch my weight, Mrs Harris, I'm afraid. Could you find time to come along to my office for a little chat — when you're not so busy?"

Gwyneth Harris smirked, looking round to make sure her minions had heard how she'd been singled out by the new sister. Very important she was, look you!

"Three o'clock, Sister, I'll be there."

"Thank you, Mrs Harris, I'll expect you then."

Conscious of the many eyes on her, the food felt like chaff in Sally's throat and she left the canteen as soon as she could. This left her time for a short walk along to a busy general store where she bought some fruit pastilles and a colouring book for Ceri. She lifted her face to the sun, walking slowly, breathing deeply. It was good to get away from the noise of the factory, and as she gazed up at the distant mountains, Sally promised herself a trip up there at the weekend.

She was checking the supplies list when the door opened and Mrs Harris came in, her well-rounded bosom thrust out aggressively, an 'I'm standing no nonsense' look on her heavily made-up face.

"Three o'clock, Sister, I said and here I am! Now, what do you want to see me about — the dieticians' menu, is it?"

"Sit down, Mrs Harris. No, it's not about the menus; I'm sure you know what you're doing there." Sally paused. "But I do have a problem. I've had several of the men in today with stomach ache . . . " Before she could continue, Mrs Harris sprang to her feet and placing two large hands on the desk, leaned towards Sally, her bold eyes flashing, her cheeks almost purple!

"So, it's food poisoning you're getting at, is it, Sister? Well, you can scrap that idea to begin with; very hygienic is my kitchen. I'm properly trained and know my job — do you know yours?"

Her voice was shrill with anger and Sally could well imagine Megan listening in the next room, but she was far too experienced to let a loud, aggressive voice frighten her!

"From the little I've seen, Mrs Harris, I'm sure it's not your fault. Please sit down and help me sort this out — I need your co-operation . . . "

Evidently, this was the right approach. With a smug smirk of satisfaction, the manageress sat down, arms akimbo and waited, her eyes still wary.

"Now, I've checked, without letting the men know it, of course, and they all had a cold beef salad yesterday. So could it possibly be that the meat was 'off'?"

The older woman shook her head vehemently. "I'm sure not — it's all good meat we have in, fresh daily . . . "

Sally bit her lip and began again.

"When did you cook the beef? You needed it cold for yesterday's salads."

"Same as always — the day before; soon as the ovens are free. While they're still hot, I pop the joints in for the next day."

"And when they're cooked — about three hours later that would be, wouldn't it?"

"That's right," Mrs Harris nodded. "Then I leave it out to cool . . . " she paused comprehendingly.

"You leave the cooked joints out to cool and then go home; the meat's out all night?" Sally persisted.

Again Mrs Harris nodded, her lips tight and defiant.

"Always done the same, I have."

"But suppose this week the meat went 'off'? Do you think that could have happened? No fault of yours, but it might cause a slight case of food poisoning, m'mm?"

"That would be hard to prove, Sister."

"I'm not trying to prove anything, Mrs Harris, but could you arrange to have the joints put in cold storage before you leave?"

"I have enough to do . . . " the other grumbled.

"If I have your word to do so — then the matter is settled."

"All right." The other's face told Sally she had made an enemy, and she knew it wouldn't be the last time she'd clash with the truculent Mrs Harris!

She rose and went round to open the office door.

"Thank you, Mrs Harris, I'm sure I can rely on your co-operation."

The older woman tossed her head and stalked out muttering;

"They should have had a nice Welsh girl for the job — folks from over the border think they know it all, but just you wait and see . . . "

In spite of her message, the night shift first-aider, Idris Williams, had not been in to see her. Well, he would just have to carry on as usual; she would see him tomorrow night — she'd had quite enough for one day! Locking up the drug cupboard and her desk, she put out the post for collection and followed Megan down the corridor to the car-park.

"Had a long day, Sister?"

"Oh, hello, Mr Jones," she turned to see the Security Officer smiling down at her. "Yes, quite a day."

As she turned her car slowly out into the road, she saw Megan picked up by one of the firm's lorries.

Myfanwy Hughes looked a little tired, but there was a mouth-watering smell coming from the kitchen.

"Special treat, Sally, on your first day; steak and mushrooms. Shall I do you some chips?"

Sally grinned with pleasure. "M'mm, why not? And how's the spotty daughter?"

"Oh, she's got a friend in — both got German measles, so they're company for each other."

"I'll pop up and see them, shall I?"

Taking the picture book and the sweets, Sally ran lightly up the steep staircase. Two small girls scrambled back into bed, eyes watery, faces flushed, but neither very bothered as they thanked Sally for her gifts.

"See you both in the morning." She blew them a kiss. "Be good to your Mum, Ceri, these stairs are tiring."

After their meal, Sally and Myfanwy sat in the snug kitchen chattering about her first day at the Works. It seemed Myfanwy knew most of the people Sally mentioned; she was soon to learn that in this little close-knit community, everyone knew everyone else, and was interested in the smallest details of each other's lives.

"Watch out for that Gwennie Harris — a nasty bit of work, she is. Man-mad too, I reckon."

"Man-mad!" Sally's eyebrows raised. "Isn't she married?"

"She is, but her man's only interested in rugger and beer, and she flirts with all the men in that canteen."

Not wishing to listen to the gossip, Sally changed the subject quickly.

"Heard from your husband, Myfanwy?" She was dismayed at the look of unhappiness that crossed over the other's face. Tears were glistening in Myfanwy's eyes as she shook her head.

"Tell me, pet," Sally coaxed softly, sorry for this homely young woman.

"It's this job, see, Sally. We — we're drifting apart all the time. When he comes home, well — he's out drinking with his mates; wants to see them all the time. I understand that, but he leaves me here alone and I want to be with him. It's as if I'm not good enough for him now." She bit her lip, her hands twisting in her lap. "I — I think he's got someone else up there; he hardly seems to want to come home to me and Ceri. Oh, I don't know — we don't seem to talk to each other any more!"

Sally couldn't help her; she hadn't met the husband yet, and from past experience she knew there are two sides to every problem.

"Well, next leave, pet, I'll babysit for you. We'll dress you up, do your hair and you can go out together. Now — let's do the dishes, and Myfanwy . . . " Sally paused, smiling, "No more chips after tonight. You can lose a few pounds, while I'm keeping mine off, m'mm?"

"Oh, Sally, I'm so glad you're here . . . "

To her dismay, Richard Llewellyn caught up with her in the corridor the next morning. Fine start to the day, she thought ruefully! Nevertheless, she bid him a cheerful —

"Good morning, Mr Llewellyn — lovely day."

"Is it? Let's hope it stays that way." Sally shrugged her slim shoulders, turning to the door of the Medical Unit, but before she could open it, a long arm shot out. Startled, she turned, just a few inches away from the broad chest of the tall figure barring her way.

"I hear you had words with our canteen manageress yesterday, Sister." Sally's mouth twitched as she looked up into his dark eyes.

"Bad news has good legs around here, Mr Llewellyn!"

"That's as maybe, but remember one thing — it's easier to get a new nursing sister than a good canteen manageress." With that he swung away, leaving Sally fuming with anger.

"Damn the man!" What was there about him that roused her temper every time they met?

Megan Evans was late again, and when she did arrive, her eyes were bleary and she looked as if she'd just scrambled out of bed and tumbled into her clothes.

"Megan — one moment, please. Close the door; we might as well get this straight from the beginning. I *won't* stand for your coming in late every morning."

As the young nurse made to protest, Sally held up her hand.

"The next time you're late, Megan, you can report to the PO's office. Now shall we start?"

For the rest of the morning, Megan's face was set and sulky, but Sally had made her point and meant to stick to it. As she went through to a small examination room, she stopped, her glance taking in the rumpled couch there.

"I thought we left this ready changed and clean for today?"

"Yes, Sister, we did."

"And Idris Williams has his own place for first aiding, you told me?"

"That's right."

"M'mm," Sally pursed her lips. Perhaps she'd made a mistake; it was only a moment's job to replace the paper sheet and pillow cover with fresh ones.

During the very busy morning, she found Megan chatting to someone on her office phone, but thinking that one ticking-off was enough for one day, she refrained from commenting. All the same, Megan seemed somewhat furtive as she hurriedly replaced the receiver, and Sally wondered if her call was to do with the lorry driver?

Then all other thoughts were driven from her mind as a young worker was brought in, covered in blood, the tip of a finger almost severed. When the stitching was completed, Sally turned to Megan.

"Thank you, Nurse, you worked well there," and saw a flash of appreciation on Megan's face. She was quite a pretty girl when she smiled, Sally thought, as she made out the triplicated forms. Dai Jones would need to look into this one; the young chap had obviously been working his machine without the safety guard in place! He would be off work for a few weeks now, but the hospital would see him before then.

Her next patient was a shy young girl

from Accounts; she had a bad migraine and Sally knew it was no use questioning her at present.

"A dark room and a quiet lie down, pet. Here's a tablet to help. And go home at lunch-time if it's still bad," she murmured as she tucked the hapless victim beneath a blanket on the couch. Then drawing the blind, she left her. She made a note to check the girl's diet; perhaps there was something that triggered off the wretched attacks.

Almost immediately another young girl came in — a very different type it seemed at first glance. Sure of herself, a regular know-it-all sort, she complained of being sick. No — she hadn't eaten the cold beef salad, and as Sally questioned her gently, she wondered if the girl was possibly pregnant? Again she made a note — 'could be pregnant' — determined to keep an eye on the girl.

If only she and the PO were on better terms, for Sally was fast coming to see how important it was that they collaborated over most of her cases. Again she sighed — it was no use, she and the po-faced Richard Llewellyn would have to have a confrontation sooner or later. And it was something she wasn't looking forward to a bit!

"Is this yours, Megan?" The bracelet she had found on the washbasin looked valuable. "You'll lose it if you're not careful. Is it real gold?"

Megan snatched it hurriedly and clipped it round her wrist.

"Of course it's gold — a present from my boy-friend, it is."

"One of the firm's lorry drivers, isn't he?"

Megan's face flushed as she nodded, and something in her manner bothered Sally, but in the next few minutes, things became very hectic. Several men had been hurt by a load of metal becoming loose from the slings of a crane. A few cuts and bruises mostly and with a good deal of cursing as they blamed the fork-lift driver. But as he was also among the injured, it was all taken in good part. And Sally found herself amazed at how casually these hard-working men regarded their day-to-day risks.

"Suppose I'll have Dai Jones breathing

down my neck?" the crane driver grumbled.

"Sorry, but I have to report all accidents."

"I know, *cariad*!" he replied good-naturedly. "Still, I think he's too worried at the moment about . . . " he looked up and saw Megan was listening intently, and he shut his mouth abruptly.

The surgery seemed quiet and empty once they were through with the last batch, and then the phone rang. It was the PO, his deep voice quietly remote.

"Sister — that chap you sent for tests yesterday — the hospital have just rung up. He *is* an epileptic. Lord knows how he got through, but I'm putting him permanently on another job where he can't do much harm. Er — thanks for finding out . . . "

His gratitude sounded so grudging that Sally found herself putting in —

"Quite! Well thanks — you'll be getting an official report from the hospital no doubt," and the phone went dead, leaving her with a little glow of triumph spreading inside her.

"What's the matter, Dai?" The Security

Officer's face looked worried and he frowned before answering Sally's query.

"Nothing to worry you about, lass," he began.

"Sometimes it helps to talk . . . " she encouraged.

"That's true. Well, it seems I've lost ten tonnes of scrap metal."

Sally's mouth widened. "How?"

"We're ten tonnes short and I've signed for it, so I'll be on the carpet."

"How on earth can you lose ten tonnes of scrap metal?"

Dai Jones grimaced and shrugged his shoulders, a defeated look about him.

"Oh, it's all a fiddle! Yes, someone's working a fiddle with their delivery notes. We're short — the scrap's being dropped somewhere else. A damned fiddle and someone's lining their pockets. But I'll get them, don't worry," he muttered to himself.

Sally was fast learning that his job was not just one of checking the workpeople in and out with just a matter of the odd scrap of metal being taken home. But ten tonnes! Poor Dai — she hated to see his pleasant face so worried-looking.

That night she found that the two little girls were over the worst of their German measles, and she persuaded Myfanwy to go and visit her mother.

"I'll read to them for a while and then wash a few smalls, so no need to hurry back, love."

"Thanks, Sally, you're a real pal . . . "

Once her chores were finished and the youngsters finally asleep, Sally sat and wrote two letters — one to her parents and the other to Roz, her ex-room-mate. Already it seemed ages since she left Birmingham and St Christine's.

The next morning, she again found the examination couch rumpled as if someone had lain there during the night! According to the night shift first-aider, her couch hadn't been used by any of *his* cases. Puzzled, Sally changed it again ready for Doctor Thomas's session. Suddenly, as she worked, the door burst open and a breathless workman, his shocked face pale, gasped —

"Sister, come quick! It's my mate . . . "

With Megan at her heels, she hurriedly followed the man through the shearing department to where a little band of workmen stood round a man slumped on the floor. He was obviously in great pain, for beneath his normally florid-looking skin, his cheeks were ashen as he struggled to get his breath.

"Here — help me get him on to this bench . . . " With a sweep of her arm, Sally cleared space enough. "Open that window and stand back." Willing hands helped her to lay the suffering man on to the bench, and she felt for his pulse. She couldn't raise a beat!

Without pausing, she leaned over and then with a hard, determined blow, struck the broad breastbone sharply. Then, for what seemed ages, she leaned over, two hands flat, one over the other, jerking hard in regular motion, up and down, up and down, with the perspiration starting on her forehead.

She kept it up until at last she could feel his heart flutter feebly at first and then take up its own beat once more. The pulse rate was poor, but at least Sally could feel it again, and she straightened her back painfully, almost on a sob of relief.

Megan had returned with some pillows

and a blanket and helped Sally to make him more comfortable. She had also prepared the shot of morphia the man needed to ease the pain of the coronary thrombosis.

"The ambulance's on its way, Sister," and with a competent look on her face, she pushed back the ring of curious workmen. With her fingers still checking the man's feeble pulse, Sally nodded.

"Thank you, Nurse," and once more it flashed through her mind that Megan was good in an emergency. If only . . . ?

By the time the man was in the ambulance and on a resuscitator, Doctor Thomas had arrived for his surgery. Sally sank gratefully into her chair, pushing her cap back from her damp forehead.

"Just had a cardiac," she announced tersely. "Silly man's car broke down. It seems he'd been pushing it over one of your hills and then, when it wouldn't start, he hurried all the way to work. Overweight and unfit . . . " She flexed her shoulders, the strain of the past half-hour showing on her face.

"Here, Sally, drink your coffee; you look as if you need it!" The sympathetic concern on Huw Thomas's face revived Sally more than the warm drink. She was fast getting to like this softly spoken Welshman, and she knew he felt the same towards her. And he'd called her Sally . . .

The phone rang — it was Dai Jones, ringing her from the gatehouse.

"Have you got a Cy Williams on sick parade today, Sister?"

Quickly she consulted her list.

"No — sorry, Dai — have you lost him?"

"His missus is here asking to see him. He should be at work, but I can't find him." Sally heard him chuckle. "He'll have some explaining to do, Sister. She's as mad as hell about something."

"Sorry I can't help," she replied. "Try the PO's office."

"No, lass, I won't bother him," and the phone went dead.

The doctor's surgery was a short one that morning, and Sally wanted his advice about one of her stomach pains patients.

"I thought it might be a gall bladder, Doctor, but I see from his notes he's already had a barium meal test. I'm wondering . . . " she paused, knowing from experience that some doctors didn't like a nurse suggesting her own diagnosis. "I thought possibly it might be an hiatus hernia."

"M'mm, let's have him in, shall we?"

A few minutes later, after the man had been examined, Huw nodded.

"I'm inclined to agree. We'll have him scanned, shall we?"

An hour later, he signed the last chit and leaned back in the chair.

"That's the lot. Now . . . " he paused and Sally saw a faint colour stain his cheeks. "I'm wondering if you'd like to come with me to a concert on Saturday night? In Cardiff at the new Saint David's Hall?" He waited and the rather anxious look on his face decided Sally —

"Yes, thanks, Doctor, I'd love to." Her answering smile lit up her lovely face, and the watching man wondered how it was that this beautiful girl hadn't been snatched up by now?

"I'll pick you up, Sally. And — can it be Huw, except for surgery times, m'mm?"

"Thanks, Huw," she replied softly.

The concert was excellent; the wonderful Welsh voices rising to the ceiling of the large hall, and Sally sighed with satisfaction as she slowly sipped her sherry in the interval. The bar was crowded and she was glad of Huw's protective arm across her shoulders.

And then she saw it . . . towering above the crowd was the dark head of Richard Llewellyn, deep in conversation with a young woman at his side. As she watched them together, a tight lump rose in her throat, making it hard to breathe. So the PO was not a woman-hater.

"It's just me he dislikes," she thought miserably, and suddenly all the pleasure seemed to drain out of the evening.

As they made their way back to their seats, Sally, trying not to stare too obviously, saw the girl turn round. Oh, she *was* rather plain! Surely not at all the sort of girl to attract the good-looking Richard? And somehow the thought gave Sally a faint glow of comfort that she couldn't quite explain.

In the car going home, Huw reached

across and patted her hand.

"I have enjoyed this evening, Sally, have you?" She nodded, beaming happily.

"Very much. Thank you for taking me, Huw."

"Any chance of our repeating the outing?" She could feel the tension as he waited for her answer. Why not? He was a nice man, and it was good to have a friend.

"Every chance in the world, Huw," she replied softly.

And when he gave her a gentle kiss — that's what it was to Sally — a kiss of friendship . . .

"Yes, I've got a map; I shan't get lost, Myfanwy. Stop worrying; I'll get a pub lunch . . . "

That Sunday morning Sally decided to drive as far as possible up the winding lane climbing up towards Twym Barlym — the mountain that overlooked the town on one side; recognizable by its curved shape at the very top — said by some local wags to resemble a reclining woman's breast — complete with nipple peak!

58

Leaving the car beside the shale path, Sally started to climb uphill, and the rocky terrain, grass tufted in parts, bare scree in others, took her on and upwards. The air was chill beneath the clear sky, and all around was the lush smell of earth and growing things. Overhead a wild bird was singing as if its heart would burst. It was good to get away from the town and people and sickness — alone with her thoughts . . .

As she climbed, a small dog on sturdy legs, suddenly broke off from his investigation of a rabbit hole and bounded across to greet her. He was a handsome Welsh corgi, and Sally grinned down at him, ruffling the deep fur round his neck. With no tail to wag, he was vigorously shaking his rear end like mad.

"Oh, you're a lovely thing, aren't you? Who do you belong to?"

"He's mine, Sister."

Startled, Sally gazed up into the dark eyes of the man towering above her. She hadn't heard his approach, but she'd noticed before that Richard Llewellyn moved like some soft-footed jungle creature. She swallowed hard, her cheeks flushed by more than the mountain air.

"Oh, good morning. I — I didn't see you . . . " She stooped to pat the little dog once more. "Please — call me Sally — out of the office, that is. It's so much more friendly." There was the hint of a plea in her soft voice.

"Miss Wakefield will do," he replied tersely. At his churlishness, her colour deepened, and she gently nudged the dog at her feet.

"Well at least he's more friendly than his master!"

"That's funny — he's usually such a good judge of character too." The cold reply made her eyes prick with tears.

"Tell me, Mr Llewellyn, are you a woman-hater or is it just me you dislike?"

"I like most females . . . " and at that Sally remembered the girl with him the night before.

"You're married then?" The words were out before she could stop them. He turned and they continued the gradual climb uphill.

"No, I'm not married. I nearly was once . . . " As he paused, Sally couldn't help asking —

"What happened?"

"She left me at the church — practically! Left me for someone older and richer — and fatter!" he added viciously.

No wonder he was so contemptuous of females, she thought.

"I saw you last night at Saint David's," she went on, "with a girl."

He halted and turned towards her, his dark eyes watching her face with a strange intensity.

"My sister. Have you seen her before?" Puzzled, Sally shook her head.

"No — I didn't know anyone round here before I came . . . "

"She lives on the outskirts of Birmingham."

"Birmingham's a big place." She couldn't quite follow what he was getting at, and to cover the pause, she went on — "Doctor Thomas took me to the concert; it was great, wasn't it? All those lovely voices . . . "

"Thomas? You like doctors, do you?" Again Sally was puzzled by something in his manner.

"Most of them. It's important Doctor Thomas and I work well together. I — I wish *you* weren't so hostile towards me. We shall need to confer closely on a good many cases . . . "

Again there was a soft plea in her voice. Switching at the tough grass with the dog-lead in his hand, he said slowly —

"You and I can never be close, Sister Wakefield."

"Why?" Sally's hazel eyes widened in dismay. "Why can't we? What have I done to make you dislike me so?" Her heart felt like a solid stone inside her.

"It isn't what you've done to *me*," he began heatedly and then, as if changing his mind, "it's no use going into it now." He swung swiftly round and called to his dog.

"See you Monday. Good day, Sister."

And with that, he strode forcefully away, the small dog struggling to keep up with him, and Sally watched them go with hurt and dismay clouding her lovely eyes.

"He's mixed me up with someone else, he must have," she told herself. That was the only thing she could think of to explain Richard Llewellyn's queer behaviour.

But somehow the loveliness had gone from the day; the sun seemed not quite so bright, the sky not so blue . . .

Deep in thought, she turned and walked slowly down to her car. Why had the PO changed his mind — for surely he'd approved her appointment in the first place? With an exasperated sigh, Sally turned the little car and drove downhill to find somewhere to lunch.

The old inn in the next village was a cosy little place; passing the rather noisy bar, she turned into the dining-room and was immediately charmed by the sight of the log fire in the hearth, its flames flickering light on the brass urns and the dark oak settle. Most of the tables were already occupied and as she looked round, a man called out —

"'Morning there, Sister." She smiled her reply although she couldn't remember his face, but then Dustrax Limited was a large firm. Immediately there was a buzz of conversation around her and she heard someone on her left say —

"Plenty of good Welsh nurses we have, look you."

Coming on top of Richard Llewellyn's

churlish behaviour, a wave of desolation passed over Sally and she bit her lip to stop its trembling. She turned to stare out of the window, waiting for the waitress to bring her food, and catching sight of the blue-hazed mountains, the little row of miners' cottages sloping step-like uphill, she vowed to stay and make these people accept her. After all, it was only the odd one or two who resented her, wasn't it?

The next morning, she found a long, rambling note on her desk; it was from the officious Idris Williams. Struggling to decipher the sprawling words, Sally's lips twitched with amusement as she read the message. He had discovered the reason for her crumpled couch! Keeping careful watch, he had interrupted a 'love-making session'. One of his young machine minders, missing his girl on the long night shifts, had found a way to see her and enjoy a stolen cuddle!

"I suggest we change the lock, Sister. I have reported the chap to the PO," the note finished.

In spite of the nuisance they had caused her, Sally couldn't help but feel a wave of sympathy for the young couple, and hoped that Richard Llewellyn would, too!

She was perturbed to find that there was another batch of 'stomach pains' in the queue. Several of the men had suffered the same symptoms over the weekend, and she hated the thought of tackling the blonde canteen manageress again.

"There's only one thing for it, Sister." Huw Thomas frowned over the notes the following morning when three more men had reported in with the same trouble. "We'll have to take blood samples from the kitchen staff."

"You mean — there could be a carrier?"

"Yes, and until we find that carrier, we'll never stop the trouble. I'll get on to the Personnel Officer," he added.

Sally's heart sank at the thought.

"Do we have to bring him into this, Doctor?" Huw's brown eyes searched her face.

"You two don't seem to be hitting it off, Sister. Why?"

Sally shrugged her shoulders.

"I don't know. It's something he's got against me, and I don't know just what it is." The regret in her voice made the watching man frown. He didn't know which he felt more — dismay at the two staff members being at loggerheads — or delight that she hadn't fallen for the good-looking PO!

The following day she and Megan were busy taking blood samples, carefully labelling the phials, trying not to disrupt the kitchen work too much, soothing the fears of the nervous ones, and trying to pacify the belligerent Gwyneth Harris.

"Trying to make more work for herself, she is," she was heard to mutter. "Nothing wrong with my kitchens."

Sally had spent an exasperating ten minutes trying to explain that there might be a carrier amongst the staff, but Mrs Harris was rude to the point of insolence, though Sally noticed she had been fulsomely agreeable to the PO!

Nevertheless, Sally didn't envy him his job when, a few days later, it was finally discovered that a young girl, recently set on, was the carrier contaminating the food, whilst not showing any signs of food poisoning herself.

From past experience, she knew that it was more than likely the girl would get another job in catering and cause the same trouble elsewhere!

"You look tired, Dai; anything the matter?" The Security Officer shook his head, perching himself on the corner of Sally's desk.

"Nothing more than usual, Sister, just . . . " he broke off as the door was suddenly opened with a jerk and Richard Llewellyn came through, his face like a thunder cloud!

"There you are, Jones, I'm looking for you."

"Oh?"

"Remember a woman asking at the gate to see her husband — Cy Williams?"

Dai Jones nodded, his eye steady.

"Well, you damned fool, you should have kept your mouth shut!"

"I don't follow . . . " said Dai, and neither did Sally.

"Apparently, Mrs W suspected Cy of two-timing her, and when you told her he wasn't at work, she went and caught him with his lady-love! Now Cy's breathing down my neck with all sorts of dire threats. He's a shop steward, too!"

The grin on Sally's face broke into a deep chuckle, and at that Richard Llewellyn turned on her angrily.

"Of course, you would think it funny, wouldn't you? Unfaithfulness in marriage is just a big joke to you!"

She gasped, recoiling from his anger as if he'd slapped her face. Dai Jones put in — "Eh, steady on, Richard, my lad. There's no call to go for Sister like that."

"No, you're right, Dai. I should've tackled you about this in my own office, but it's no laughing matter." He swung round to face Sally, "and just remember, Sister, be careful when trespassing into personal matters of the staff. Their health is all you're concerned with."

Anger flamed into Sally's cheeks, her eyes blazed as she faced him.

"Quite, Mr Llewellyn. You would do well to remember that, too, and try to keep your resentment of me out of our day-to-day working. I know my job — you don't have to preach to me. Now, may I get on with my patients, please?"

She rose and flung open the door, her breasts rising and falling rapidly as she tried to control her anger. This man was always making things difficult for her, wasn't he?

As he followed Dai Jones, Sally thought she caught a swift glimpse of respect in the PO's eyes, but she could have been wrong. All the same, she was not going to take his hostility lying down, she told herself angrily.

It was a pleasant change to have the friendliness of Huw Thomas, and after surgery they spent a few minutes over their coffee.

"Sally, would you come out to dinner with me tonight after evening surgery?"

Seeing the look on her face, he hurried on —

"With one of my partners and his wife — make a foursome?"

Sally saw the sense in this arrangement; it wouldn't do for them to be seen out together too often yet. In this tight-knit community, gossip spread like wild fire and a doctor had to be careful. She saw the mute appeal in his brown eyes and suddenly, with a smile, she nodded —

"Thank you, I'd love that, Huw. Will you pick me up or shall I meet you?"

"Bless you, Sally," he reached over and gave her hand a squeeze. "Perhaps it would be wiser if we all met up in the foyer of the Westgate Hotel, m'mm? I'll book a table for eight-thirty."

The pleasure on his face made Sally wonder if she was doing right to accept his invitation? She liked Huw very much; she badly needed a friend after Philip's defection, but it wouldn't do to let him get too fond of her, would it?

As she sat there, the image of Richard Llewellyn crossed her mind; what on earth had he meant by that remark about her chasing doctors? Later when she took a batch of notes into his office, he thanked her coolly and then added —

"You'll have no more trouble with your — er — couch, Sister. I've transferred the young Romeo to day shifts."

Sally couldn't hold back her smile and she was surprised to see the answering grin on his face. 'Oh, he should smile more often' she thought breathlessly. The way his eyes crinkled, the creases dimpling the corners of his mouth, made him look so much more attractive, and the breath tightened in her throat.

"Thanks, I needn't change the lock then. I *did* feel a bit sorry for them . . . " she paused, at the change that came over his face then.

"I doubt that he'll thank us after a few years of wedded disharmony," and with that he shuffled the notes on the desk.

Sally flounced out of the door. Well! the thaw didn't last long, did it? Pity. 'I could like you, Richard Llewellyn, if only you'd smile more often'.

"You look lovely, *cariad*." Myfanwy watched as Sally finished her make-up. The deep rose-coloured silk dress clung lovingly to her slim figure, and with a final touch of toning lipstick, Sally turned and thanked her young landlady. Her only jewellery was a pair of chunky gold ear-rings, and she reached over for the little fake-fur cocktail jacket. Nothing would induce the soft-hearted Sally to wear real fur, but looking through the mirror, she decided that she didn't look too bad at all!

71

It was obvious that Huw Thomas thought the same. As he greeted her in the old-fashioned foyer of the town's oldest hotel, his face lit with delight. And once again Sally wondered if she was doing right to date this nice man? She didn't want to get too deeply involved. She turned to greet Huw's partner and his wife. Frankly curious, they made her warmly welcome over pre-dinner drinks in the crystal-chandeliered lounge.

"Thank heavens for our emergency call service. At least we can get the odd uninterrupted night out." Huw stretched out his legs and leaned back, enjoying the comfort and the company.

"Amen to that, Huw," the other doctor echoed, raising his glass.

At that moment, Sally, glancing round with interest at the red plush and heavy gilt furnishing of the lounge, caught sight of a face she knew. What on earth was young Megan doing here? Surely it was a rather expensive place for a lorry driver to afford? Sally was surprised to see how very well-dressed Megan's companion was; his suit and toning shirt were of the finest quality.

"Isn't that our Megan?" Huw leaned forward speaking quietly into Sally's ear. She turned and saw the same quizzical questioning in his eyes. She nodded and suggested softly —

"Perhaps a special celebration . . . ?"

"Could be," he agreed.

Throughout the enjoyable meal, Sally's thoughts kept returning to the enigma of Megan and her boyfriend, and then she turned to answer the inquisitive doctor on her right. She was still surprised by the direct manner these Welsh folks asked leading questions. That it was genuine, friendly curiosity she soon came to realize; still it shook her when she caught the drift of the conversation. Huw's friends were obviously trying to do a bit of match-making and were hoping to discover if she was suitable and willing enough!

The twinkle in Huw's eyes told her that he knew all too well what was happening, and later that night, as he drove her home, he asked —

"You didn't mind, did you, Sally? All those questions — it's just folks' way down here — friendliness, you know?"

"I'm getting used to it; everyone knows everything about everyone else it seems." She paused, "Still I hope your colleague and his wife didn't think we're . . . ?"

He reached across swiftly, touching her hand, before he drew the car into a dark lay-by.

"They know I've been lonely since my wife died, Sally," he began. "It's three years now, and since our son went away to college, it's been worse."

"Tell me about her." She saw his knuckles gleam whitely as he grasped the wheel.

"I should have known — I blame myself, but I was the last to know — too late! She died of cancer and I — who try to heal everyone else's wife — could do nothing to save her."

The rawness of his voice told of his bitter suffering.

"No one can take her place, but life must go on, and all my grieving won't bring her back. And I know she wouldn't want me to be alone." He drew in a deep breath and turned to the silent girl beside him. "Till now I didn't even consider marrying again. But now . . . "

"Don't say it, Huw — please. Let us just be friends for now."

He drew her close and gently placed his lips on hers.

"For now, Sally my dear, but I'll live in hope."

She reached up and touched his face and he covered her hand with his, then placed a kiss in her soft palm and closed her fingers over it.

"Friends — for now," he murmured.

And Sally sighed as he started up the car and drove her back to Caradoc Terrace . . .

"Goodnight, Huw, thanks for a lovely evening." She watched as he reversed and drove away — a feeling of misgiving in her heart.

Moving quietly through to the kitchen, Sally stopped, surprised to see her landlady crouched in a chair over the dying fire.

"You've been crying, Myfanwy!" The young Welsh girl's face was red and swollen, her eyelids puffed. As Sally looked at her, her lips quivered in distress.

"What's happened, love? Is it Ceri?"

75

3

CONCERNED, Sally asked quietly, "Want to tell me about it?"

Myfanwy gulped, screwing her damp hankie into a tight ball.

"No, I can't," she sobbed and then suddenly turned and faced Sally. "I must tell someone or I'll go crazy . . . "

Drawing up a chair, Sally sat down waiting, watching as the distressed girl tried to pull herself together.

"It's about Terry, my husband. Things haven't been too good between us lately; I wanted to have another baby, he wants to earn more money first. So he took this better job — away from us. But when he comes home, he doesn't seem to want me as much. He's no letter writer, and I've been worried he's found someone else up there."

She paused and the tears sprang to her eyes once more. Sally reached out to give her a tissue and put a soothing hand on her arm.

"Go on, pet," she urged, feeling there was more.

"This morning, I had a letter from Edinburgh — from a girl." Myfanwy's voice choked. "Oh, Sally, what shall I do? She — she says she's expecting his baby . . . "

She buried her face in her hands and sobbed bitterly, while Sally struggled to find words of comfort.

"You must write to Terry — give him a chance to tell you his side. Please, Myfanwy, don't do anything silly until you've heard from him."

It was some time before she managed to get the heart-broken girl to bed and her promise to write Terry first thing in the morning. Unfortunately, he had no home leave due, and Sally's heart ached for the anxiety Myfanwy would have to go through before then.

She undressed and lay on her back staring up at the ceiling, her thoughts chaotic. The enjoyment of the evening had been somewhat overshadowed by the sight of her young nurse and the lorry driver spending money so extravagantly, and now Myfanwy's distressing news . . .

Sally put out the lamp, trying to settle to sleep. Strangely her last conscious thought was of a smile transforming the stem face of a tall, dark-haired man — a smile she knew she'd do almost anything to see again . . .

Sally waited to see if Megan mentioned anything about the night before, and when she didn't, decided not to bring it up herself. The less she gossiped about her date with the doctor the better, and when the rather shorter sick parade was over, she told Megan —

"I'm going to pop into the hospital and see our cardiac case, Megan. You'll manage all right, won't you? I won't be long."

She found her patient sitting up and joking, looking much better. Pleased to see her, he was soon giving her the medical history of all his ward mates! Finally, as she rose to leave, she told him:

"I must go now; glad to see you looking so much better. They miss you at the works . . . "

"Aye, I bet I'll find a right cock-up,"

he agreed with a shake of his grey head. Sally laughed, patting the hand lying on the bedcover.

"You just take it easy; let 'em suffer." Promising to come and see him again, she turned down the ward, amused by the long, low whistles that brought back sudden memories of St Christine's.

She barely had time to button on her white dress when a workman came dashing into the waiting-room, his eyes wide with shock.

"Come away quickly, Sister — it's young Jones the tenor — lying on the floor, he is — in a pool of blood." So thick was his accent that Sally could hardly understand him.

"Where?" she asked briefly, picking up the emergency kit.

"In the bogs — the toilets, Sister. My, he looks real bad . . . "

"Stay here on duty, Megan. I'll send for you if I need you. Now," she turned briskly to the man, "lead on . . . "

He was right — Jones the tenor did look bad! His fair hair lay in a pool of blood, his young, grease-stained face pale with a bluish pallor round the mouth. Checking his pulse, she rapidly swabbed away the dirt from round the broken skin, cutting away sufficient hair to leave the contusion clear. The actual wound Sally left — the blood was already starting to clot and a firm pad would suffice until the patient reached hospital. His pulse was not too bad; he was a strong young chap and in no real danger. He'd certainly have a sore head for a day or two, she mused.

Having despatched the workman to instruct Megan to call an ambulance, she made the young man as comfortable as she could, and then had time to look round.

With the usual strong urinal smell, the whole toilet block was none too clean; cigarette ends and litter blocked the drains, paintwork peeling, and the floor . . . she paused and for the first time noticed a large patch of oil beside the patient's prone figure. Curious, Sally rose to her feet to take a closer look. Clearly then she saw the imprint of a man's foot . . . the cleats of the boot's sole and heel still showing in the patch of oil.

Stooping, careful not to tread on it, Sally was able to decipher a number — a four and a two — and yes, a seven. 427! That wasn't a size surely? she asked herself.

Then to her horror, she saw what had caused the injury! Someone had hit the poor young chap with the short length of metal tubing now lying bloodstained in the gully — the trickling water around it stained pink. Sally knew better than to touch it . . .

As she moved back to her patient, the door clanged open. It was Richard Llewellyn.

"What is it, Sister?" Anxiously, he bent over the figure lying so still on the tiled floor.

"Bad laceration, concussion — the ambulance won't be long."

As the PO straightened his back, she pointed to the gully.

Look — there, that's what did the damage, I reckon."

Grim-faced, his swift glance took in the sight of the weapon.

"A police job, I'm afraid. They'll get their chaps on to this."

Sally could tell from his voice how loath he was to bring in outsiders, but just as she was about to agree, there was a faint groan, and the youngster's eyes flickered and then closed again.

"No — no police." The words came with difficulty and he was unconscious again. Sally waited, seeing the conflict on Richard's face.

"I'll wait till he comes round before telling the police . . . "

"But . . . "

"I'll shut the water off — leave that there. Perhaps he'll give us a clue. I'd rather sort this out ourselves if we can. I'll get on to his relatives . . . " and with that he hurried off as the stretcher-bearers came in. Sally had the toilet block locked and an 'Out of Order' notice pinned on the outside door.

She found the Security Officer already waiting in her office. The Works grapevine worked even quicker than that at St Christine's, she mused, as she began to tell Dai Jones what had happened.

Pensively pulling at his chin, he murmured:

"Wonder who did it; it's going to be

hard to prove unless the young man saw whoever hit him."

"Dai," Sally began slowly, "do all the men wear special boots here?"

"Boots?" He looked puzzled. "Why, yes, they're standard issue. You know the type of thing — special hard toe-capped safety boots — compulsory wear here."

"M'mm," she thought aloud, "and are they numbered on the bottoms, I mean?"

Dai Jones' brow knitted as he recalled —

"Yes, they are. Why, Sister?"

"Someone — with large feet and number four two seven on the bottom of his boots was in that toilet block this afternoon — unless it was the victim's footprint I saw in the pool of oil on the floor." She looked at the Security Officer. "Can you find out, Dai?"

He nodded. "Easy — there'll be a record. I'll get on to it." He paused in the doorway. "Bright lass, you are . . . "

"I could be wrong, Dai."

"We'll see, Sister."

She was in the canteen for a cup of tea a while later, and Gwyneth Harris's hard blue eyes were full of curiosity.

"Someone hurt in the gents' loo, was there, then?"

On her guard, Sally shrugged off the question nonchalantly.

"Someone slipped on the wet floor. Nasty bump and a bad headache, that's all."

Done out of a choice bit of gossip to spread, the buxom blonde slammed down the cup of tea, and then with a sickly smile, asked Sally —

"Enjoy yourself last night, Sister? The Westgate's a posh place, isn't it? Still I don't suppose the doctor's short of cash, is he?"

The look from Sally's angry eyes should have silenced the manageress, but she was a hard case, and her simpering snigger showed that she'd scored again! Not much happened in and around Dustrax Limited that the nosy Gwyneth didn't come to know about. And she was always on the look-out to stir up a bit of trouble, especially to those who didn't kowtow to her!

Megan seemed in a hurry to get off duty that night.

"Going somewhere nice?" Sally asked. For a second, Megan's eyes were wary, then she confided:

"To that new night club out at Usk; got a good cabaret and a smashing group."

Sally bit her lips; Megan was young and wanted to enjoy herself, but . . .

"Don't forget you're supposed to be studying, Megan," she pointed out. The young nurse's face flushed.

"If I don't go with him, he'll take someone else."

Sally frowned, wishing she could gain Megan's confidence. Her lorry driver certainly earned a good wage! All the same, too many late nights wouldn't do Megan's career any good.

That night Myfanwy told her —

"I couldn't wait for an answer to my letter, Sally, so I rang him."

"You can do that . . . ?"

"Yes, by ship to shore radio — for emergencies. They didn't like it, but I finally convinced them I *had* to speak to Terry."

"What did he say?"

"That it — it could be possible — what

the girl says." The words fell flat and heavy between the two girls as they sat either side of the kitchen table.

"Sally — it's like a nightmare . . . " heart-brokenly the words poured out then in a torrent. Apparently, Terry and some of his mates had wined and dined too well on an overnight leave to the mainland alongside the oil rig where they worked. Drunk and hazy, he had woken up the next morning in a sleazy, grubby room, with an equally sleazy-looking girl bending over him. He had woken up with a splitting head and no recollection whatever of what had happened! It was a familiar, sordid story, but when it involved someone you knew . . .

"How could he, Sally?" Myfanwy sobbed. "He — he says he still loves me. He's in an awful state — blames himself bitterly — says it's never happened before . . . "

"Do you believe him, Myfanwy?" Sally asked gently.

"I don't know. I feel that I'll never trust him again. How could I after this? I wanted another baby — he said to wait, and now . . . " Her sobs filled Sally with pity, and she wondered what she could possibly do.

Then she thought of something that might help.

"Why don't you go up and see this girl, Myfanwy?" Two red-rimmed eyes looked up, in surprise and then with a glimmer of hope.

"See her? Oh, I couldn't . . . could I?"

"Yes, you could!" Sally answered firmly, "And I'll go with you!"

"Going somewhere special?" Richard Llewellyn's eyes questioned as Sally told him she was going away that weekend — and might be late back on Monday. She nodded, reluctant to say more.

"To Birmingham — to see someone special?" he went on relentlessly. Again Sally didn't reply — let him think what he liked!

"I'll probably be back in time, don't worry," her voice sounded cool. "What I came in to see you about is — will you call in to see my two cases in the hospital? The heart case and the young chap with concussion. I don't suppose either will be discharged before I'm back."

"I was going to drop in to see them anyway. I want to see if he knows who coshed him — and why?"

She rose and collected her notes.

"You can have your weekend away without any qualms, Sister."

"Right," she answered tersely, barely concealing her anger, "that's settled. See you Monday." And she only just managed to resist the childish temptation to slam his office door behind her!

They left a delighted Ceri with her doting grandmother, and took the train northwards early on Saturday. As they sped swiftly towards Crewe, Sally found that she was reluctant to see the back of the lovely Welsh mountains and valleys. The industrial Midlands and then the Black Country seemed so flat and uninteresting. If only some of her new colleagues were nicer, she knew she could well lose her heart to that corner of Wales.

Myfanwy sat tense and miserable, her

brown eyes full of apprehension. To take her mind off the coming ordeal, Sally began to tell her about some of the hair-raising things that had happened during her years at St Christine's — humorous things as well as tragic ones; of the happy comradeship of Roz and her set; of the terrible blunders they had all made in the early days of their training.

"You'll be missing your friends then, Sally?" Myfanwy's voice was soft with sympathy, and Sally nodded.

"M'mm, I do. Still . . . " she brightened, "I've made new friends already. You and Ceri." She reached across and squeezed the other girl's hand. "And Doctor Thomas and your Dai Jones," she continued, and then wondered what Myfanwy would say if she knew her lady lodger would gladly give anything for the friendship of one dark-eyed man — a man who seemed to dislike her so much!

"Let's get some lunch, shall we?"

Seated in the comfortable dining-car, Myfanwy murmured —

"It's costing you quite a lot, Sally — train fares and so on . . . "

Sally, about to pass this off, noticed

the other's face and grinned widely.

"Tell you what, landlady, you can knock something off next month's rent." Myfanwy sighed with relief and agreed; Sally noticed that she hardly touched the food the efficient waiter set before her.

At long last the train pulled into the old-fashioned station at Edinburgh.

"We'll have to take a taxi. Got the address?"

Quickly Sally bustled Myfanwy towards the taxi-cab rank — the sooner this awful business was over the better . . .

"You're sure this is the place, lassie? It's no' the sort of district for two young ladies like you." The taxi driver shook his head, his thick Scottish voice tinged with worry.

And as they left the tall granite buildings and shops and made their way deeper into the derelict-looking slums round the docks, Myfanwy's eyes grew wide, and Sally couldn't help sharing her dismay.

"Oh, this is horrible, Sally," she whispered. "Is this the right place?"

The taxi driver nodded reluctantly.

"Shall I wait for ye?"

"No thanks — we don't know how long we'll be," Sally told him.

He frowned, shaking his head again.

"All the same," he said, "I'll be back in half an hour. Mebbe you'll be ready for me by then."

She thanked him warmly, grateful for his concern. She didn't relish the idea of going into the grim-looking tenement building at all . . .

"To think of my Terry here!"

"But he was drunk, Myfanwy," Sally reminded her as she urged her forward. "Come on, love."

The smell inside was overpowering; it was fusty, dirty, reeking of cabbage, stale smoke — and mice! Outside No. 6A, with its peeling paintwork and a cluster of unwashed milk bottles, they both stopped and looked at each other with misgiving. Myfanwy looked so scared so, taking the lead, Sally braced herself and knocked on the door, and then knocked again — louder.

"A'right, a'right. I'm not ruddy-well deaf!" The door swung open and a man stood there, bleary-eyed, his dirty shirt open to reveal a thick neck and a dark, hairy chest. He looked down at them, his close-set eyes belligerent and wary.

"Yes?" he barked. "What d'you want? Getting me out of kip an' me on nights an' all . . . "

"Sorry," Sally apologized briefly. "We — er — came to see Liz Buchan. Miss — er — Mrs Liz Buchan?"

"What d'you want wi' Liz?"

Sally looked round and began again — "May we come in? We can't very well talk here, can we?" She had already sensed the eyes that were peering through a slit down the side of the next apartment's door.

The man hesitated and then possibly also aware of the inquisitive neighbour, he grudgingly opened the door. Once inside, he turned and called loudly —

"Here, Liz — you're wanted . . . "

If the landing was bad, the room was even worse; dirty, unkempt and again that awful smell blending the stale reek of smoke and spirits.

Then Sally was stunned by the sight of the girl slowly coming through from another room, and heard Myfanwy's breath catch too.

"Liz Buchan?" she asked and the girl nodded; the dirty light showing the overbleached, unwashed hair. In spite of her grubby, loosely-fitting smock, Sally's professional eye estimated that she was about seven months pregnant! And she realized this at the same moment as Myfanwy, as she heard her gasp —

"Oh, but — it was only about eight weeks ago when Terry . . . it can't be . . . "

"Here, what d'you two want, eh?" The man's truculent voice held a threat and, swallowing hard, Sally showed him the letter, held carefully at arm's length.

"You must recognize the writing . . . "

And as he grasped the situation, he turned to Liz with an angry growl, and to their horror, gave her a resounding blow across the face!

"You bitch! You've been at it again, ain't you?" His torrent of abuse made the girl cringe, and Sally and Myfanwy stood there trembling for her.

"'Course the kid ain't your husband's.

She was just trying it on. Hoping to get some money out of him, I reckon. Just a set-up between her and some of her tarty mates . . . "

"Shut up, you fool! He'll pay — just to keep me quiet, I bet."

The venomous look Liz gave the man made Sally shudder, and she longed to be out of there — in the fresh air away from the sordid scene. Then to her surprise, she heard Myfanwy's voice, firm and unafraid.

"He won't pay, you know! And if *we* hear one more word from either of you, I'll go to the police. In fact, I think I'll take this letter to show them anyway. Blackmail, they call it." Turning to Sally, she said quietly, "Come on, Sally, let's get out of here."

She gathered herself together as if the very air was contaminating.

"Hey — wait!" The man's voice held a different tone then. "The police! Say — there's no need to bring the cops into this. I'll deal with her . . . He jerked a grubby thumb in Liz's direction. "She won't be bothering you again — I'll settle her . . . "

To their relief, the kindly taxi man was waiting outside for them as promised, and Sally asked him to take them to a decent little hotel for the night.

Once settled in a clean double room, Myfanwy slumped on her bed, pale with released tension, and Sally wisely decided to say nothing more until they had both had a wash and a meal.

"Let's have a bottle of wine, shall we? I reckon we both need it." Sally was pleased then to see the Welsh girl eat a good meal. Sipping her second glass of wine, she began —

"How can I thank you, Sally?"

"By forgiving Terry. Talk it out with him. Better still, don't wait till his next home leave — I should write him a nice long letter. Tell him about that dreadful place we went to today. Give him a chance to tell you his side of it." She paused seeing the pensive look on Myfanwy's face. "I bet he never even touched that awful Liz — it was just a set-up." She managed a faint laugh. "Oh, I reckon he's learned his lesson all right, Myfanwy, my love."

"I'll forgive him because I do love

him so, but it'll be hard to forget, I'm thinking," Myfanwy replied quietly. "But I'm beginning to feel certain that it was only a set-up, as you call it. I remember now — Terry protested over the phone that he'd been robbed — that's how that woman got his address." She shuddered. "Oh, Sally, that wretched place . . . what a way to live!"

"Try to forget it, pet," Sally begged her. "Put today behind you; give Terry another chance."

Back in their room, it wasn't long before Myfanwy's steady breathing told Sally that she was asleep, but the thoughts buzzing round in her own head kept her from dropping off. She wondered if Richard Llewellyn had learned more about the young workman's assailant? If only she could have told him about her discovery — but then he would probably have laughed at her — or told her to mind her own business!

She punched her pillow and tried to settle to sleep, determined not to give up trying to win over young Megan and to solve the puzzle of the lorry-driver boy-friend; determined to discover what the PO had against her.

"Look, Myfanwy, how about this for Ceri?" It was fairly early the following morning. After a quick breakfast they had settled their hotel bill and made for the station. Sunday trains were not so frequent, and it threatened to be a long and tedious journey.

Stopping at the newspaper kiosk for magazines, Sally saw an attractive little doll dressed in red tartan and white frilly blouse; it was sure to please Ceri.

"You'll spoil her, Sally," Myfanwy smiled, looking so much brighter, as if a load of worry had been lifted from her shoulders.

They sat waiting for their train on the chilly platform; the mornings were getting cooler as autumn grew nearer.

"By the way, my mum thinks we've been off on a weekend trip together — for pleasure." Myfanwy made a wry grimace. "Some pleasure trip! Oh, Sally, I'm so glad you came to live with us — you're such a pal!"

Sally squeezed her arm.

"Glad I could help, love, and don't

worry — I won't breathe a word to anyone about this." She paused and then went on tentatively: "Can I suggest something?" Myfanwy's eyes widened as she waited. "Well, I'd like to — er, take you in hand a bit. How can I put it?" Sally hesitated. "I'd like to slim you down a bit, pet; put you on a strict diet until Terry gets home. What do you say? Let's knock his eye out with a new you, m'mm? Get your hair done, some new clothes, and then when he comes home, I'll take Ceri off your hands — stay out of sight while you both have a grand time together."

Myfanwy's eyes were shining — seeing just how it could be — how she longed for it to be!

"Oh, Sally, if only we could make a new start . . . "

"Leave it to me." Swiftly and impulsively Myfanwy hugged the other girl just as the train drew slowly up to their platform.

Once in their seats, Myfanwy murmured, "It won't be easy, Sally, I do love my food, but it'll be worth it, won't it?"

Ceri was delighted with her doll.

"I've got something for you, Aunt Sally." Excitedly she brought forth a crumpled paper napkin and unfolded it carefully.

"They're Welsh cakes, see? Gran let me make them for you on her bakestone."

"M'm, I must try one, they look scrumptious." And Ceri watched as Sally tasted the flat round scone with a welcome mug of coffee.

"Are they — scrumptious?" Two anxious eyes watched her face.

"Absolutely lovely, pet. Thank you. And do you know, Ceri," Sally added solemnly, "these are the very first Welsh cakes I've ever had!"

The little girl leaned fondly against her knee.

"I'll make you some more soon, shall I?"

"Yes, please. But Ceri, I wonder if you'd show *me* how to make them?"

Myfanwy thought her young daughter would burst with pride as she nodded her head in agreement. Dear Sally, she ought to marry and have children of her own. Doctor Huw wasn't too old to start another young family, was he?

As she drove through the big iron gates the next morning, Dai Jones touched his cap and passed her a slip of paper through the car window.

"Good morning, Dai. Getting a bit chilly now, isn't it?"

"Chilly?" He looked surprised and then laughed. "Just wait till there's four feet of snow, Sister; it's right lovely yet, it is." Looking at the slip of paper, he nodded. "That's the information you wanted, Sister. See you later about it, I will."

"Thanks, Dai. After surgery will be best . . ."

She inched the car forward, conscious of the stream of vehicles piling up behind her.

For once Megan was there before her, and the pleasure Sally felt was reflected in the warmth of her greeting. But the young nurse's face wore a strained, worried look, and Sally knew that a confrontation with her junior was fast approaching. Before opening the mail, she glanced at the note Dai Jones had given her. It said simply

— "Boots No. 427 were issued recently to Taf the tube."

Puzzled, Sally knitted her smooth brow, and then screwing up the paper, she threw it into the waste basket. There was just time before surgery to go along to the PO's office, and as she did, she was surprised at the sinking feeling in the pit of her stomach — or was it her heart that felt so heavy? As she reached the door she paused and straightened the pert little white cap that sat so cutely on her smooth chestnut hair. Then pulling back her slim shoulders, she knocked and entered.

"Good morning, Mr Llewellyn," her voice was pleasant but cool.

He raised his head from the pile of papers before him, and two dark eyes took in the slight figure standing stiffly there. Just for a brief moment there was a touch of pleasure in those eyes and then it was gone.

Morning, Sister. So you're back then? Had a good time in Birmingham — get what you went for?"

If she hadn't known differently, Sally would have thought he really was curious about her weekend, but why? She passed the tip of her tongue over her dry lips.

"I wondered — did you see the two chaps in hospital?"

"I said I'd go, didn't I?" The ice was back in his manner, and she told herself she must have imagined the spark of warmth she saw in his eyes a moment ago! Sighing softly, she said —

"You did, yes. How are they, Mr Llewellyn?"

"Your heart case is doing fine; he'll need a few weeks off sick, and then a lighter job." He shuffled his papers. "I'm arranging to send him and his wife to a convalescent home we use, and then putting him in the stores as a control clerk. He'll be taking an earlier retirement, too."

"Thank you — and the young concussion . . . ?"

"He's round — with a sore head, moaning about the patch of hair you cut away! Fancies himself a bit of a Don Juan, that one." There was a hint of a smile playing round the PO's firm mouth, and for a fleeting moment, Sally wondered what it would be like to be kissed by that mouth! The thought made her blink; she'd never find out, would she? Quickly she brought her attention back and asked —

"Did he see who attacked him?"

Richard Llewellyn shook his head. "He knows all right, but he's not saying. Just adamant that no police are brought in. Says he'll deny everything if we do! So it will have to rest there. He'll be discharged this morning, and as soon as his stitches are out, he'll be back at work."

"It won't rest there," Sally told herself stubbornly. Still she wasn't saying a word to the stern-faced man on the other side of the desk.

"I've let the authority know about our canteen carrier; I doubt if she'll work with food again," he finished firmly.

Without thinking, Sally burst out —

"You sound so hard. The poor girl's got to find work . . . "

Two eyebrows, like black question marks, told her that she'd put her foot in it again!

"You — a nursing sister — must know what havoc that woman can cause in a works' canteen. Of course she can't find a similar job; she's a danger to everyone, but there are other jobs. I gave her a good reference — said she was a hard and willing worker . . . "

He was right, of course, but all the same Sally hated his unbending manner.

"Anything else?" In an attitude of dismissal, he returned to his papers.

"No, thanks, Mr Llewellyn," she replied and flounced out of his office. If she had glanced back, she would have been surprised at the look on Richard Llewellyn's face at that moment . . .

"Can I come in, Sister?" Dai Jones poked his grey head round her office door as she finished her notes for the morning's surgery. There were quite a number of cases she meant to keep a close eye on.

"Come in, Dai. Megan's making a cup of coffee." The big man eased his bulk into a chair, then stirring his third spoonful of sugar into his steaming coffee, he began —

"Well, Sister, I think we've got the culprit, don't you?"

"We can't be sure . . . "

"It all fits — and I reckon I know why

Taf did it." He paused to take another sip of coffee. "He has a daughter, and young Mike is a bit a lad for the girls; plays the field, he does. Well, Taf's a chapel-going man; strict and self-righteous, he is. So — where do we go from here . . . to Mr Llewellyn?"

"Oh, no!" Sally's face flushed and she bit her tongue on the hasty words. "Er — no, Dai. I've a feeling he'd laugh at us." She paused, twisting her pen between her fingers. "What if we wait till Mike comes in to have his stitches out — then I could perhaps have a little chat with him; see if I can get to the bottom of the incident? I don't want to bother the PO — not without something more solid to go on."

"Just as you say, Sister. Perhaps young Mike will open up to you a bit. As I said, he's got an eye for a pretty girl."

"Flattery will get you everywhere, Dai Jones — you and your lovely Welsh accent . . . " She laughed up at him and saw an answering twinkle in his eyes.

4

"YES, that's looking fine. How's the headache, Mike? All gone?"

Chatting casually, Sally deftly removed the last suture.

"No headaches, Sister — good solid stuff my head. It's the bald patch I don't like!"

Dai Jones was right — this young man did fancy himself, but why not? He had a firm, lithe figure, handsome face with a ready smile that showed off his strong white teeth. A little brash and too sure of himself, but the years would cure that!

Before seeing him, Sally had asked Megan if she might borrow her small tape recorder. She'd had an idea and was now hoping it would work. The tape recorder was hidden in a desk drawer, with the little microphone placed carefully among the odd bits of surgical equipment on the desk top. Now all she had to do was coax the young concussion case to talk!

"It'll soon grow again, don't worry,"

she replied. "You shouldn't have turned your back on Taf the tube, should you?"

Mike leaned back in his chair, looking at her with a wry twist to his lips.

"So you know?" he accused softly.

"Yes, I know — and strictly between ourselves, Mike — why did he cosh you?"

He frowned. "I don't want to get old Taf into trouble."

"Then talk to me, if not the police. I don't think you can pass this off as easily as that, my lad."

"I suppose not." He rubbed his hand over his chin, trying to make up his mind. "Well, Taf has a daughter, see? She's — well, she's such a plain and homely bird . . . " he broke off, his cheeks colouring with embarrassment. "Lord, how can I put it?"

"Go on," Sally encouraged softly.

"Well, she fancies me no end — chases me all the time! Honestly, Sister, every time I turned round, she'd be there — every disco, every pub . . . "

He swallowed hard and then went on —

"At first, I sort of felt sorry for her

— she doesn't seem to have many mates or fellas — she's so plain and gawky."

"And . . . ?"

"Well, one night, just as I was chatting up a really lovely bird — up comes Taf's daughter and sort of stakes her claim on me. So, of course, the other girl dropped me like a brick. And I was hopping mad; told her to get lost in no uncertain terms." He shuffled remorsefully in his seat. "I was sorry afterwards. I could tell she was pretty upset. And that's not all — she must have already told Taf a tale because last week he followed me into the toilets and goes for me, good an' proper!"

"Didn't you try to explain to him?" Sally asked.

"I did, but he was so blazing mad — reckoned I'd played fast and loose with his daughter. Ready to walk her down the aisle, he was, I reckon. Well, when I turned to wash my hands, something bashed me over the head — and I passed out."

"So he came prepared to beat you up?" Sally asked in dismay.

"No — that's not it! He's not a bad

bloke — bit of a bible-thumper, but not a bad workmate. So — no cops, no fuss! Perhaps I asked for it," he fingered the wound gingerly. "I should have made it plain from the start, but I was sort of sorry for her."

"And I bet you enjoyed the adulation," Sally thought to herself, reaching surreptitiously to switch off the tape recorder.

"OK if I let the PO know something of this . . . ?" she queried.

Mike jerked to his feet angrily.

"You promised — in confidence . . . "

"If I quietly put it to Mr Llewellyn — put him in the picture . . . it'll go no further, I promise you. You can trust *him*, can't you. Without his word on it, I won't tell him anything, so . . . "

She could see he was weakening, and before he left her office, she had his consent. As soon as she was clear of the Medical Unit, she gathered up the tape recorder and marched along with it to Richard Llewellyn's office.

Calmly, she placed it before him.

"Will you listen to this tape, Mr Llewellyn? It's in the strictest confidence, I've given my word on that. It's Megan's machine, so I must return it soon."

Puzzled, he nodded.

"Will do — give me a few minutes . . . "

She had just finished dressing a deep gash on a workman's leg when the PO came storming in, the tape recorder in his hands. Taking her time with the bandage and the necessary notes, she waited until her patient had closed the surgery door behind him, and then went through to her office.

She glanced across at Richard Llewellyn's broad back as he stood looking at a DHSS pamphlet on the wall. Something told Sally he wasn't really taking it in! He turned to face her, tension in the air between them.

"Just what do you think you're playing at, Sister?"

The words dropped like hard pebbles and Sally's heart began to thud beneath her white dress.

"I should have thought that tape spoke for itself," she answered calmly. "Sit down, please — I hate having to look up to you."

With a faint snort of derision, Richard

sat down, his face like a thunder cloud.

"How did you get on to Taf the tube?" he asked. Quietly, Sally explained about the patch of oil, the decipherable figures left behind by Taf's safety boot. She made it sound so simple, and this infuriated him more than ever she could tell!

"And why wasn't I told of this — why go to Dai Jones, when it was so obviously my territory?"

Sally's even white teeth bit her bottom lip, her eyes troubled.

"I thought you'd laugh at me, tell me it wasn't my business."

"Well, it's not your job — it's mine!"

At that she really lost her cool.

"So that's it; you just hate me to succeed in solving a problem, don't you?" She banged her palm on the desk top. "It's no use — this constant tug-of-war between us, Mr Llewellyn. My patients and your cases will all suffer in the long run. What does it matter who sorted this business out?" she finished, sickened to her stomach by the conflict, but determined not to be put down by this — this pig-headed man!

"Is it so hard to work with the proper department — or do you think you nurses know it all?" he jibed.

Had Sally known it, he was finding it more and more difficult to sustain his annoyance with her. She looked so beautiful when she was angry; her soft cheeks were flushed, her eyes wide and her lips trembling. But some devil, some inner knowledge drove him on. Just as his last remark about nurses made Sally blow her top!

"Nurses know it all! Huh! I reckon if Florence Nightingale had ever worked with you, she'd have thrown her lamp at you!" she stormed.

For a split second the words hung heavily and then, as she blinked away the angry tears, she heard his faint chuckle. She looked across at him warily and saw that his face was creased with laughter. The laugh lines round his eyes, the softening around his mouth, for a moment turned him into someone she could like very much.

"Oh, Sally, what shall I do with you?"

Surprised at the turn of events, but still flushed with anger, she replied swiftly —

"See Taf the tube. What a funny name! Tell him what you've learned from that tape. Get him to make it up with Mike; we can't have the men going around coshing each other, can we?"

He rose, nodding his agreement.

"Keeps you busy though, doesn't it — doing your job and some of mine!" With that parting shot, he left Sally sitting there, bewildered, remembering his laughter — and that he'd called her Sally . . .

"Really had a battle in there, didn't you?" Sally looked up from her notes and shrugged.

"I've had better relationships, Megan. We don't seem to get along, the PO and me."

"I think he's rather dishy, so do all the office girls. Not that he ever looks our way," Megan mourned, then changed the subject. "By the way, Sally, that chap you were sewing up just now . . . "

"What about him?

"Well, that's the third time he's been in lately."

113

"Must be accident prone," Sally suggested.

"Funny thing — I checked last time — he always uses his safety guard. One of his mates hinted that he had domestic troubles though."

Sally looked up into her young assistant's face.

"I've said it before — you're a good nurse, Megan. One of the most promising I've ever worked with. Thanks, I'll keep an eye on him . . . "

Megan's face crimsoned with delight and there was a feeling of warmth in the air as she prepared to close down the surgery. Sally noted too that Megan was being more meticulous in her cleaning-down these days. She closed her book firmly, saying —

"At least it's been nothing worse than cuts and bruises! By the way, Megan, if you need any — er — help with your exam work, I'm willing to help you any evening . . . "

A shadow passed over the girl's face. "If you want to, that is," she finished lamely.

"My boy-friend likes to see me most

nights." There was almost a tinge of regret in Megan's reply; Sally knew she ought to be studying some nights at least, but it was a pity to spoil the closeness that had just grown between them.

"Well, goodnight, Megan," she called lightly as she turned to lock the drugs cupboard.

That evening, she dressed with great care. She was going to Huw Thomas's house for the first time and felt nervous. Huw had often spoken of his housekeeper, Anna Rhys, who seemed to rule his home with a firm hand. She wore a fine wool dress in a shade of peacock blue and knew it suited her well. She kept her make-up light, and apart from her gold hoop ear-rings, wore no other jewellery. Telling herself that she was silly to feel so tense, she picked up her car keys and went downstairs, calling a goodnight to Myfanwy as she did so.

It was a beautiful night — barely dusk with a crisp smell of autumn in the air. The leaves on the trees were turning all shades of bronze and yellow and gold. Sally stood for a moment breathing in the fresh air. The bracken on the mountains was already curling and brown-tipped, and the thought of seeing them in winter was pleasant, as was that of spending a congenial evening with Huw. His last surgery done, they would have a meal at his place for the first time.

Sally was surprised at the size of the house. With its overhanging eaves, huge bay windows and large pillared front door, it was rather an ugly place. Even with a tidy front garden and neat gravelled drive, somehow it didn't look very friendly. Certainly not for the amiable Huw, she thought, as she waited for someone to answer the heavy bell.

If the house wasn't too prepossessing, well — neither was the sight of the tall, gaunt woman facing her then. Her grey hair pulled back tightly into a bun, her putty-coloured wrinkled face was far from welcoming. Deliberately she kept Sally standing there while she looked her slowly up and down. Sally resisted the temptation to reach up to a strand of wind-blown hair, and kept her gaze cool and steady.

"Sister Wakefield?" Sally nodded.

"Come in, please."

"Good evening, Anna — lovely evening, isn't it?" She kept her voice light and pleasant, determined not to let her misgivings show.

"Sally — hello, my dear." There was nothing cool about the welcome Huw Thomas gave her, although she noticed that he waited until the formidable Anna had taken her coat and ushered them into the lounge before kissing her cheek.

The lounge was large — big and sombre and hideous. The walls were dark, so were the heavy pieces of furniture, carpet, covers, and the long French windows were concealed by net curtains and thick brown velvet curtains. Something of what she was thinking must have shown on her honest face, and seeing it there, Huw looked round disparagingly.

"I've been meaning to get something done about it, but . . . " he paused and Sally blurted out —

"But Anna wouldn't approve!" Her hand flew up to her mouth in dismay. "Oh, Huw, I'm sorry. I shouldn't have said that."

He lead her to the hard settee and turned to the drinks table nearby.

"You mustn't mind Anna. She's been with us for ages; was with my late wife's family before we were married. Since I've been alone, she's taken over completely. Deep down, she's a good soul."

"She's afraid I've come to upset the *status quo*." From beneath her lashes, Sally glanced up at him as she sipped her drink.

"And have you . . . ?"

"M'mm?"

"Have you come to upset the *status quo*?" He sat down beside her, his eyes serious as they scanned her face. "I hope so, Sally my dear, because I'm getting very fond of you, you know."

He'd said fond — could she settle for fondness? But look what falling in love with Philip had brought her? The hesitation was just a fraction too long, and Huw picked up her hand and gave it a warm squeeze.

"Don't worry about it now, Sally. Just let me see you now and again. Who knows, I might get to grow on you?" he grinned.

She returned his smile, and reaching across to cup his face in her hands, she placed a soft kiss on his cheek.

"Like a fungus, m'mm?" And they both laughed companionably.

To her vexation, Sally caught sight of a hovering figure over Huw's shoulder, and she dropped her hands hurriedly.

Huw reddened like a naughty schoolboy.

"Anna — I didn't hear you come in . . . " The housekeeper gave an audible sniff.

"Evidently!" she replied tersely. "Food's ready," and she left them to follow.

"Oh dear," Sally couldn't restrain the chortle. Really, the woman was like a character out of an old-fashioned play.

Huw's arm held her close and comforting, and then she saw his face fill with anger as his eyes surveyed the long table in the equally cheerless dining-room. The housekeeper had set their two places miles apart — one at each end of the very long table!

"This is ridiculous." Angrily Huw scooped up his place setting and plonked it down next to Sally's. "There, that's better."

All through the meal, Anna made her disapproval obvious, and Sally was thankful when it was over.

"Coffee in the lounge, please, Anna," Huw requested.

"And I'll pour," Sally told herself, determined not to let this disagreeable old biddy have it all her own way! Resuming her seat on the settee, she placed a small table beside her knee.

"That was a very nice meal, Anna, thank you. Put the coffee here and I'll pour." Without giving the dour old woman time to demur, she added, "Two sugar and a little cream — that's how you like yours, isn't it, Huw?"

"Please," Huw nodded. Manlike, he completely missed Sally's assertive little ploy or the disapproving scowl on his housekeeper's face.

Comfortably, like two old friends, they chatted as they drank their coffee, and Sally urged him to tell her more about the town, the valleys beyond, and the people who lived there. She felt she had so much to learn — there was so much she didn't know, wasn't there? Times were still difficult for these people, for as exhausted mines closed there were no new industries to give them new jobs, and this part of the country had the highest unemployment figures.

She could see that Huw cared deeply and longed to help the folks and the town where he'd been born and bred. Suddenly, the persistent ringing of the telephone interrupted their conversation.

"For you, Doctor. There's an emergency at the Works," Anna Rhys' face was even more glum as she made the announcement.

"I thought I heard a fire engine a few minutes ago . . . " Sally recalled and dashed through into the hall at Huw's side, to stand anxiously watching his homely face grow more and more grave. Issuing a few terse instructions, he added:

"I'm on my way . . . " and replaced the receiver. "Get your coat, Sally — we're needed at the plant. There's a serious leak from the big acid tank."

In a few seconds, they were in his car covering the short journey to the Works where they could see the flashing lights of the fire engine; men scurrying across the yard in grotesque-looking respirators. Dai Jones saw the car and hurried to meet them.

"Glad to see you, Doctor — you, too, Sister."

"Any casualties?" Huw wasted no time as they dashed towards the Medical Unit.

"Mostly from the fumes. I've sent for more cylinders of oxygen."

"Good man."

Already the men inside were coughing and spluttering and gasping as they reached out for oxygen masks. Red-rimmed, streaming eyes turned gratefully, and Huw and Sally lost no time in trying to relieve the men's misery. Several had skin burns from splashes of acid on their hands and legs.

"Lots of water . . . " Gently they swabbed the burns again and again, letting the sterile water soothe and weaken the effects of the deadly acid.

"I must see if they need me out there. These chaps'll be all right now, Sally."

"I'll come with you." Ignoring his warning, she followed him into the works.

They found men in respirators struggling

to stop the flow of acid coming from a leak in the bottom of a wall, while others played a fine spray of water constantly on them and the surroundings. The pungent fumes were acrid and Sally found her linen surgical mask no use at all. Someone supplied Huw with a respirator and signalled her to go back.

Regretfully she realized she'd be no use if her own eyes and hands were affected. She raced up to the canteen and snatched up teapots and mugs; those men would need tea — lots of it, before the night was through. As she loaded a tray, she heard someone behind her.

"Two minds thinking alike, Sister? Here give me that — you grab some tea, sugar and so on . . . "

It was Richard Llewellyn, and for a moment Sally stood staring at him. She'd never seen him before in shirt sleeves, without a jacket and tie, and the sight of those muscular arms, lightly covered by fine dark hairs, caught her glance and held it. There, just the two of them, alone in the dimly-lit canteen kitchen, she could feel her heart throbbing with something more than the drama of the moment. Richard paused in the process of stacking rows of mugs, and without looking at her, urged —

"They'll be needing this down there — come on." Dumbly, she obeyed him. Why was it that she could never be in contact with this man without her pulse racing, her heart beating faster? Was she afraid of him and his bitter tongue? Yet, somehow it wasn't fear she felt right then — just a sense of rightness that they should be here working together . . .

Back in the Medical Unit they got the kettles on to boil.

"What's happened out there?" Sally asked after they'd given the men hot tea and sent home those who were all right.

"There's a huge tank holding thousands of gallons of acid, used in the treatment of metals and so on. It's inside that bund wall — the protective wall," he paused and stirred his tea. "We had some workmen in yesterday renewing one of the pipes. Apparently, they must have breached the wall and the trickle of escaping acid became a flood."

Just then two firemen came in, removing their respirators; both had slight acid burns on their hands, and as Sally treated them, Dai Jones hurried in.

"Ah, good lass, tea. I'm parched; can't stand these damned masks, can't seem to breathe in 'em."

"What's happening now, Dai?" She could see how worried he was for this was his department's responsibility.

"I've rigged up emergency lights. I'm arranging for more drums and pumps; that tank's got to be emptied before we can work on the breach. Need a new wall, too."

"And the acid that's escaping?" she asked.

"Got on to the ICI for more alkaline powder. We'll then be able to neutralize the acid. At the moment, we're hosing it down — but it's affecting the sewerage mains and the local chaps are breathing fire down my neck!"

"Oh, Dai — here let me swab your eyes, they look a bit sore."

"I'm all right, Sister, I must go . . . "

"Me, too." Richard Llewellyn had been collecting mugs, heaving more oxygen cylinders into place and helping Sally generally.

"You!" Suddenly Sally was afraid for him and that was silly. He knew what he was doing; he must have seen many such mishaps in the works before. Why didn't she want him to go out there?

It was a long night, and in between patients, Sally made stacks of notes, brewed copious gallons of tea, washed burns, bathed streaming eyes, passed around the oxygen masks to ease laboured breathing . . . Huw had been in and seeing that she was coping had to leave. He had a heavy surgery session as well as a round of house calls — all before coming back to the works.

Before leaving, he dropped a light kiss on her cheek. Too bad that at that moment, someone came through the office door, needing a pair of dark eyes swabbing.

"Sorry!" Richard Llewellyn apologized tersely.

"It's OK, I'm just going. Ring me if you need me, Sally."

Two minutes later, Sally found her normally steady hands trembling slightly as she gently swabbed the PO's red-rimmed eyes. They were so close she wondered if he could hear her heart thudding?

"Getting very chummy with our local doctor, aren't you, Sister?"

Sally held his jaw firmly with one hand whilst thoroughly rinsing an eye with the other.

"Just friends, that's all. Not that it's any of your business." Anger at the effect his nearness was having on her made her snap back at him.

"You're right — though I don't think you two should go around kissing — not at work, I mean."

She jerked his chin sideways to swab the other eye. It was so hard to avoid looking at him when they were eye-to-eye like this!

"There you are — all done." She turned to replace the bowl and suddenly felt her elbow gripped by a strong hand.

"Don't I deserve a kiss, too, Sister? I've been a good patient . . . " and before she could reply, he lowered his head and covered her lips with his; gently at first and then more firmly. Shocked for a second, she resisted fiercely, and then as the tingling warmth from his seeking lips spread through her body, she weakened and found herself responding with a fervour she had never experienced before. Struggling back to sanity, remembering who he was and how he hated her, she pushed frantically, turning her face away.

"You — you'll be sorry in the morning you did that!" she choked angrily, though the anger was aimed at herself as much as him.

"But I enjoyed it and so did you. Must go now and see if I'm needed. There'll be reams of blasted forms to fill out after this little caper . . . "

And with that he left, leaving Sally's lips smarting, tingling with the remembered touch of his, and how wonderful they had felt.

It was almost dawn when she finally begged a lift back to Caradoc Terrace, leaving a note for Megan telling her that she might just be in late. Exhausted, she fell asleep at once, only to dream vividly that she was struggling through dense clouds of white fumes, crying, calling out a name . . .

"I wish I could have been here to help

you," Megan said regretfully the next morning. Except for dark rings beneath her hazel eyes, Sally looked her usual calm, bright self. She was pleased to see that Megan had thoroughly cleaned up the place.

"I've taken all the things back to the canteen. Told old Gwyneth Harris to stop her moaning — that at least I'd washed them up for her. Was it bad, Sally?"

"No — few really serious burns, but the fumes were the worst. Have you heard how things are this morning?" Sally asked, donning her white dress ready to begin the sick parade.

"According to Dai Jones they've managed to close the breach, and the tank's almost emptied now. The first-aider coped with the odd swabbing. *I* should have been here . . . " Megan added once more.

"We managed quite well, thanks." Sally looked up, asking, "Anyway, where were you?"

At that Megan flushed, tugging at a lock of hair.

"We — er — went to a nightclub."

And then she brightened. "Very good, it was, too — we had a great time."

Seeing that they were alone, and thinking she might not have the chance again, Sally asked lightly —

"Your boy-friend must earn a terrific wage, Megan, to afford the life he leads, m'mm?"

Again Megan's colour deepened.

"He says he does a bit of moonlighting — they all do around here."

"Yes, I see, but even so . . . ?"

"Oh, don't *you* start — I get enough aggro from my parents!" the young nurse burst out angrily, and then seeing the look of dismay on Sally's face, she mumbled, "I'm sorry . . . " Turning away, her fingers idly moving the things on the shelf beside her, her voice was low as she went on, "If you must know — well, I am worried. About where he gets all his cash from, I mean. He's never short and yet he still has time to take me out most nights."

She shook her head, her eyes troubled and Sally reached across and put her arm round her shoulders.

"Don't be cross at me, love, but I

— I've got an awful suspicion that he's on to some sort of a fiddle." She felt the young shoulders jerk and hurried on, "He's up to no good; he'll involve you if you're not careful. I'm sure Dai Jones is on to his caper. Give him up, Megan, before he drags you down with him. You're too good a nurse to ruin your career now."

Megan shook her head slowly from side to side.

"Try, Megan — I know what it's like to be in love with the wrong sort of man."

Surprise crossed Megan's face at that.

"You do — what did you do?"

"I moved to come down here. It was the only thing. So I know how hard it is, but some instinct tells me that you'd be best away from your lorry driver . . . "

Just then, after a sharp rap on the door, the tall figure of Richard Llewellyn entered. He looked tired, his dark eyes were red-rimmed, his mood sombre. But remembering his kiss the night before, Sally found it difficult to act normally.

"There'll be a long sick queue this morning. Don't let anybody stay on at work with bad hands, Sister."

Sally bridled — as if she would. Then she relaxed again; the last thing he needed right then was an argument.

Fortunately, most of them were only surface burns, and just as they had finished with the last of the men, a young girl came in, her eyes wary as she looked around.

"Can I see you — alone, Sister?" she asked.

"Certainly, come in. Megan, why don't you pick up my car and pop round to see our cardiac case? He's going to a convalescent home soon. Get his home address from the file, there's a good girl."

Once they were alone, she turned to the girl.

"Let's see — it's Alison Nichols, isn't it? You came in before with — er — nausea, didn't you?"

There was a hard, defiant look in the girl's eyes; something about her that Sally couldn't quite understand.

"That's right, Sister — and as you guessed then, I'm sure — I'm pregnant!"

"I see." Sally let out a slow breath,

waiting for her to go on.

"And I want an abortion!"

"Have you seen your own doctor, Alison?"

"No — besides he's our family doctor, and I don't want my folks to know."

"I'm sure he wouldn't tell anyone. No doctor does," Sally began, only to be interrupted abruptly.

"He's an old man — doesn't really believe in abortion deep down, I suppose."

Something in the girl's eyes — or rather the way they didn't quite meet her own, made Sally ask —

"How far advanced are you, Alison?"

"Four months — just over," came the stubborn reply, confirming her own suspicions.

"Then you must know it's far too late for you to have an abortion. The hospital wouldn't do it . . . "

"It can't be — I can't have the baby. I don't want it."

"How about the father?" Sally asked gently.

"Oh, him! He doesn't want to know; it was just one of those things — just one night and I'd run out of my pills.

133

Just my rotten luck!"

Watching the wretched look on the girl's face, Sally knew she had to ignore her own feelings on the matter. She had almost burst out — 'what about the child?' But that wouldn't help.

"So — what can I do?" Was the girl really as hard as she made out, Sally wondered; was she an unfortunate girl needing help, or someone carelessly promiscuous? She knew she wasn't there to pass judgement or criticism — only to help to the best of her ability. "I'll have to find someone who'll do it, won't I? I've got a bit of money saved up."

"A back-street butcher, you mean?" Angrily Sally pulled no punches. "I'd hate to take such a risk myself. It's dangerous — for you. You could quite easily die — of septicaemia — be found ex-sanguinated, bled white — never be able to have a child later. Oh no, Alison, it hurts — horribly . . . "

Remorselessly, Sally piled on the agony; anything to frighten and prevent the po-faced girl facing her from procuring an illegal abortion!

"I *can* help you, Alison. Help you find

a place to have your baby — someone experienced in these matters to advise you. You can have the child adopted — give it a chance of a good, loving home."

"My folks . . . "

"They'll have to know soon anyway, if they haven't already got their own suspicions."

"I daren't tell them; I don't get on at home so I left," she moaned, and Sally wondered just what the girl's people had had to put up with in the past?"

Would you like me to see them?" she asked, but at that the girl stumbled to her feet.

"Oh no — I don't know! I want to get rid . . . " and with that she ran out of the surgery, leaving Sally chewing on the end of her pen. Something would have to be done — and soon . . .

5

SALLY tapped on the door nervously. It had taken her some time to make up her mind, and even now she wasn't sure whether her decision was the right one. Perhaps after all, Huw would have been the one to help her?

"Come in."

Richard Llewellyn looked up with, for a swift second, a look of warmth on his face, but at his next brusque words, she knew it was only her wishful thinking!

"I'm busy . . . "

"I want to see you, Mr Llewellyn," she began, thinking how stupid it was — this formality between two colleagues . . . and after his kiss the night before!

"I'm very busy, Sister, won't it wait?"

Shaking her head, she told him —

"No — it *is* rather urgent, and I need to discuss the problem with someone — with you. And I don't want it to stand over the weekend unresolved."

As it was already Friday lunch-time, it

136

had to be now. He shuffled a stack of notes on the desk in front of him, and gave her a rueful glance.

"Unfortunately, I'm just off. I'm chairing a meeting in Cardiff this afternoon and evening — an amalgamated PR thing . . . "

Seeing the look on her face, he added, "It isn't that I don't want to help . . . "

Sally shrugged and turned to leave.

"Sister — er — Sally, how about tomorrow?" She waited, hardly daring to breathe — tomorrow was Saturday!

"How about you and I taking a trip somewhere — say down the Wye Valley — have a bit of lunch — give us plenty of time to discuss your problem. What do you say? Bring your notes and so on . . . " he added as if to remind her that it would be a strictly business trip.

"Thank you, Mr — er — Richard," she smiled coolly, but her pulse was racing. "I'd like that very much."

"Good. I'll pick you up at say — ten o'clock. That do?"

Again she nodded, not quite able to meet his eyes.

"See you then," she agreed.

That evening, with the helpful hindrance of young Ceri, Sally washed her hair, did her nails and gave herself a facial. After the last few hectic days, she felt she needed a little self-pampering! Round-eyed and curious, the little girl draped herself over the dressing-table, watching intently as Sally started her beautifying routine.

"M'mm, smells lovely, Aunt Sally. I'm going to have some of that when I grow up."

"If you let me, I'll use some of this on your hair now, pet," Sally suggested, knowing Ceri hated her mother washing her thick curly hair.

"An' some of that spray stuff?"

"Ah-ah, the whole works. Come on . . . "

And for the next few minutes, there was a considerable amount of noise and giggling and soapy splashing around in the bathroom, until Myfanwy poked her head round the door to see what was going on.

"Oh, bless you for doing that, Sally. I hate the battle every time. By the way, I've got some news for you . . . "

It was a full hour later before a highly

perfumed and rather exhausted Ceri was finally tucked up to sleep. With her hair still in large rollers, and her nails newly-varnished, Sally was grateful for Myfanwy's cup of coffee. She could tell that her young landlady was bursting to tell her the news.

"Terry's coming home next week. I had a lovely long letter, see? And he says we are going to talk things over between us — everything. Oh Sally, I think it's going to be all right — about me starting a baby, I mean." She paused and then added in a rush —

"Shall I leave off taking my pill?" To her surprise, Sally shook her head emphatically.

"No, Myfanwy — not yet. Don't do it that way. Wait until you know that Terry really wants another child." She reached across and took the other's hand. "Don't you see, Myfanwy, if you do it like that — well, it's sort of cheating on him. Almost as bad as that awful woman up North. You must *both* want a child. He has the right to decide too, pet, don't you see?"

Sally so desperately wanted things to

go right for Myfanwy and the plea in her voice was sincere. Slowly Myfanwy agreed and rose to her feet, collecting the coffee cups as she did so.

"All right, Sally. I'll wait till he comes home. After all," she brightened, "I've waited all this time, so a few more weeks . . . "

"How's the weight, love?" Sally reached out and tugged at the other girl's waistband. "Oh, you're going down."

"Almost a stone," Myfanwy told her proudly. "When Terry's due home, will you help me — get me done up a bit — like you've done for yourself tonight?"

"Of course, the whole works, pet. We'll knock his eye out, and don't forget, I'll baby-sit."

"Bless you, Sally. Hope you have a nice day tomorrow."

A pensive look crossed Sally's face.

"I doubt it," she murmured.

It was ages since Sally had spent so much time trying to decide what to wear. Myfanwy had plumped safely for a duffle coat and sneakers, but Sally, remembering the PO had mentioned lunch, tried to think of something comfortable, yet smart. Finally, she settled for a fine wool trouser suit in light navy with a thin white sweater underneath. And to match her lipstick, she twisted a bright red scarf into a rope to tie at the neckline. Her navy kid shoes had a slender high heel, so she rolled up a pair of comfortable old flatties in a lightweight anorak and felt herself ready for anything.

The early morning sun caught the chestnut highlights in her thick brown hair, and as she went downstairs in answer to Myfanwy's call, she tried to still the rapid beat of the pulse in her throat, determined for once to keep her cool and enjoy the trip.

Richard Llewellyn's long legs, clad in light fawn cords, swung out and then he came round to open the car door for her.

"Lovely morning," the sight of him standing there, darkly handsome, his soft brown suede jacket snug across broad shoulders, a cream polo-necked sweater beneath it, gave Sally's voice a sudden lilt of happiness as she took in a quick deep gulp of fresh air.

He gave her a sharp encompassing glance.

"Lovely morning — lovely companion. You look very smart this morning, Sister Wakefield, if I may say so?"

"You may — and it's Sally, please Richard — at least for today," she entreated. With a wide grin, he settled himself behind the wheel.

"Comfortable, Sally?" he asked with emphasis on her name.

"Yes, thank you, Richard," she replied with equal stress on his, and at that they both laughed aloud and Sally, at least, felt the day had started off well. And she crossed her fingers as she hoped it would stay that way!

"How does Hay-on-Wye sound — it's a great run through narrow country lanes — with a special stop for coffee?"

She settled deeper into her seat with pleasure.

"Anywhere, thank you, Richard. I don't know any of the places round here. Hay-on-Wye," she pondered, "the book place?"

At that he laughed.

"You could say so — millions of books, in fact. But it's a nice spot for all that."

They were soon out of the town and into the narrow country lanes, and the sheer beauty of the autumnal tints surrounding them took Sally's breath away. All the leaves on the trees were turning various shades of gold and brown; masses and masses of delicately coloured trees climbing up the mountain sides.

"The loveliest time of the year," Richard agreed, although winter has a lot going for it down here."

They gradually climbed along up the narrow roads under the dark Skirrid Mountain and then stopped outside an old inn.

"The oldest in Wales, they reckon. Goes back to about eleven hundred and ten," Richard told her as he locked the car. "Interested?" his dark brows rose in query.

"Oh yes — very." Eagerly Sally's eyes scanned the old sign above the huge, heavy oak door.

"Good! The landlord's a jovial chap;

does a great pot of coffee, and if you use your charm, my lass, he'll show you round."

Glancing over her shoulder at him, she asked —

"Charm? Have I got any?" And the gleam in her eyes threw out a challenge to him.

"Yes — you've got what it takes . . . " and there was a tinge of regret in his voice, as if she was using it on the wrong person.

Inside it was old and dim and faintly musty-smelling, but as he'd said, the young innkeeper was used to inquisitive tourists, and after two cups of excellent coffee, he took them through behind the bar and upstairs to see the room reputed to have been used as a court house by the infamous Judge Jeffreys — the notorious 'Hanging Judge'.

"This bathroom was once the little cell where the prisoners were held overnight. Poor devils — they got short shift. They took them out and hung them here — from this big oak beam," the landlord pointed out. "See, them's their heel marks — made as they struggled their last!"

Sally shivered, trying to recall her schoolday's history lessons — not one of her long suits, but Richard and the innkeeper thoroughly enjoyed telling her all about the gruesome details.

"Supposed to have sentenced three hundred and thirty people to death or deportation, he did, at the 'Bloody Assizes . . . '"

The rooms were now a family guest-room and bathroom, but the sight of the sturdy oak beam with the scorch and drag marks of the rope still showing was enough to give Sally the creeps!

"See — this little pot," Richard pointed over the old original fireplace. "This used to be filled with ale and left outside for the spirits of darkness — hence the terms 'Devil's Brew' and 'to sup with the Devil'. Superstitious lot they were in the Middle Ages.

They spent almost an hour listening and looking at the ancient artefacts — all with a history of their own, and Sally's face reflected her pleasure as they started on their way again.

"Thanks, Richard, I feel I've stepped back in history for a while, but oh! I'm glad we live today and not then."

He glanced sideways at her, and as if to help her back to the present, said quietly —

"Can you tell me now what it is that's so urgently worrying you, Sally? The road's quiet — no traffic from here to Hay, so . . . ?"

With a jerk, she brought back her wondering thoughts to the problem in hand.

"It's about a girl in the Accounts Department — she's four months pregnant . . . " she began slowly.

"Alison Nicholls, you mean?" he interrupted her.

Surprised, she half-turned in her seat. "You knew?"

His lips twisted wryly. "I am the Personnel Officer, Sally! Actually another girl, a colleague of Alison's, came to see me about something or the other, and while chatting, she let out her suspicions — and I've just remembered . . . "

She should have known — he was good at his job and very little escaped those deeply penetrating eyes of his, she reckoned.

"So . . . ?" he urged.

"She wants an abortion, but, as I told her yesterday, it's too late. Briefly, she threatens to seek a back-street job — says she daren't tell her parents . . . "

"But she hasn't any parents." A frown creased his forehead. "I remember now," he began slowly, "I remember feeling sorry for her when we set her on; rotten home background. When she was a child, her father ran out on her and her mother. The mother eventually married again — to a man who didn't want the little girl, so the grandparents brought her up. They're strict chapel," he smiled ruefully, "and up the valleys that's a pretty grim scene for a lively youngster. I believe Alison left her grandparents and set up for herself. Quite, possibly the freedom went to her head and so . . . "

Sally sighed. "I don't know — I scarcely know her. I can't make up my mind whether she's a real hard case, or just a scared kid pretending to be one. But, Richard, I — we've got to stop her having an illegal abortion."

"Quite," he agreed. "What on earth made her leave it so late?"

"I did get the feeling that she thought by ignoring it, the problem would go away."

Sally moved restlessly in her seat.

"It's hard to tell — I'd have to know her better."

"You can help though, can't you, Sally — a home for unmarried mothers and so on . . . ?"

"Of course, plenty of help — if she'll let me!"

Richard negotiated a sharp bend and then slid past a loaded farm wagon, before answering.

"Let me see her, Sally, talk to her and try to get her to accept your help — above all to get her promise not to do anything stupid. No need to contact the grandparents — they can't help much, I doubt."

As he finished speaking, the car glided downhill to a big car park besides an old ruin, and Sally looked round with pleasure.

"Here you are — Llanthony Abbey and Priory ruins. Like a quick look round and then on to lunch?"

As Sally agreed happily, he suggested —

"Forget Alison's problem for now — I'll see her first thing Monday morning and see what I can do." And with that, she had to be satisfied. Only parts of the Abbey ruins, along with those of the priory and almshouses, were still standing, but across the smooth lawns a tearoom and little shop were doing good business.

Taking her arm, Richard led her across to where the high arches lined the ruined old cloisters. And what delighted Sally most of all was the beautiful view, for the lace-like stone arches framed the panorama of the half-circle of mountains in the background, making a natural, perfect picture.

Together they slowly paced uphill, taking in the crisp autumn air, their faces warmed by the bright sun, and Sally felt an agreeable sense of companionship between them as they climbed side by side over the tufted grass. Being here with this quiet man seemed suddenly so right, and she wondered what *he* was feeling just then?

When they reached the top of the steep hill, they turned to take in the glorious view below. Sally found herself breathing hard and wondered if she was possibly out of condition — or was it the nearness of the man beside her? *His* breathing hadn't altered at all.

"You're pretty fit for a sedentary working bloke, I mean. I suppose you play rugger like everyone else around here?"

"Used to, but it cost me too much time off from work getting over the various injuries, so I gave it up. Besides, I'm getting too old," he added with a grimace. "Do a bit of refereeing for boys' and youth clubs — that keeps me fairly fit. Right now all this fresh air's making me hungry. Come on . . . "

He took her arm and tucked it under his, and his touch spread a warm glow through the whole of her body. A few minutes later, he turned into the car-park beside an old-fashioned coach house in Hay-on-Wye. In spite of the Saturday crowds, it was quietly peaceful in the quaint old dining-room, with just the faint clink of plates and cutlery. Sally shrugged off her jacket, and as she picked up the heavy leather-bound menu,

Richard told her —

"They specialize in trout here — lovely big, speckled brown ones — grilled with flaked almonds . . . "

Three ample courses later, Sally leaned back and sighed contentedly, lazily stirring the fragrant coffee before her.

"M'mm — this is one of my better days, Richard. Thank you."

"You must see Ross-on-Wye and the Forest of Dean over on the other side of the motorway," he paused and then went on wickedly, "Get your doctor to take you sometime."

Suddenly it was as if a cold chill passed over her, and to her dismay, Sally found her lovely bubble of contentment deflated. Blinking the sting of tears from her eyes, she asked huskily —

"What have you got against doctors, Richard?"

He shrugged, his face set.

"Let's not spoil our outing, Sally. Sorry I said that . . . " He rose and reached out for her jacket. "Ready?"

Pausing only while he settled their bill, Sally went out to the car. If only she knew what he had against her seeing

Huw Thomas occasionally — it couldn't possibly be jealousy, so it must be that he had a thing against doctors.

"My landlady's husband is coming home soon on leave from the oil rigs up north. I've promised to babysit for her."

Now he'd know she wouldn't be going out with Huw for a while anyway.

"You're a puzzle, Sally. You seem so kind-hearted and caring; good at your job — and yet . . . ?"

She held her breath waiting for him to go on, but to her chagrin he completely changed the subject by pointing out a passing landmark.

"And over there — that's the Brecon Beacons — now there's a sight in winter. All bleak and bare, covered in snow — almost like a moonscape. And this is Brecon town — well, the outskirts of it."

And so their desultory chat left out any personalities, leaving Sally as puzzled as ever by this man's manner.

Soon they were on the outskirts of Merthyr Tydfil — a scene of derelict mine shafts, ugly coal tips and poor dwellings, and at the sight of these,

Sally felt rather depressed. This was so obviously an area hit by poverty and lack of work. Richard explained how gradually the old coal tips were being reclaimed and landscaped.

"Not much will grow on coal slurry though."

Just then they were passing an untidy scrap metal yard, and with a sudden exclamation, he swung the car through the unhinged gates and climbed out, slamming the door.

"Wait there, Sally — I've got an idea . . . " and with that he hurried off towards a tumbledown office building.

It seemed ages before Richard came back, his face angry-looking, his lips set tight.

"By God — I was right! I did recognize some of our stuff there." He shrugged a shoulder indicating a huge pile of scrap metal — all of which meant nothing to Sally.

"That's where some of our missing scrap has got to," he muttered as he started up the engine, and suddenly she grasped what had happened!

"Megan's boyfriend . . . " she murmured.

"The young lorry driver," he gritted. "Yes, he's one of them. Just wait — I'll have their guts for garters."

"Poor Megan," Sally began, and at that he cast a quick glance at her face.

"Keep this to yourself, Sally. Don't say a word to Megan. We don't want those boyos tipped off." He sounded so hard, and she shivered in spite of the warmth of the car. But she knew he was right — those men had been systematically robbing Dustrax, and they could have got Dai Jones into trouble. They deserved to be caught. All the same, she felt sorry for young Megan.

To her surprise, Richard stopped the car beside a brightly-painted caravan in a small lay-by — a tea bar for lorry drivers.

The young chap dispensing tea from the hissing urn seemed to know Richard and they greeted each other like old chums.

"Best cuppa in Gwent! Here you are, Sally — mind it's hot."

Pleased to stretch her legs and grateful for the mug of tea, she listened with amusement as he told her of some of

154

the exploits he had shared with this young chap.

"Made redundant, so he set himself up here. Does a roaring trade, too. He's noticed our lorry going by with scrap . . . "

It was growing dusk by the time they got back to Caradoc Terrace. Sally sighed softly as she gathered up her things — sorry the day was over.

"Thanks again, Richard, for a lovely day. I have enjoyed it — honestly."

As she spoke, she felt his arm reach across her shoulders. Her heart began to beat erratically in her breast, and she knew she wanted him to kiss her. The air between them was electric; it was as if they were the only two people in the world — so close together there in the car.

"Is that all I get, Sally . . . ?" His voice was husky and low as he reached out to cup her chin.

"I — I said . . . " Before she could finish, his lips were on hers, gently at first, and then as she responded, they became more fierce in their demand.

As if of their own accord, Sally's

hands slid behind his dark head, pulling it down — holding it closer. At last he raised his head, leaving her feeling bereft; his breathing ragged, almost a groan as he straightened up and moved reluctantly away.

"Better not go any further, Sally. Thanks, too, for a good day. See you Monday," and as if he couldn't trust himself any further, he slammed the gear lever, hardly waiting for her to get out.

As she stood there, her legs feeling like jelly, watching the car move out of sight, she was thinking how different two men's kisses could be!

Sally had a lot on her mind that Monday morning. She hated the thought of wiping the happy look from her young assistant's face — longed to warn her in some way; to cushion the blow that was shortly to fall. But she also had her loyalty to the firm and Richard too — not to mention dear old Dai Jones who was being held responsible for the shortages. She kept wondering, too, if Richard would be seeing Alison Nichols soon, and how he would fare with her.

Somehow the morning seemed to drag until doctor's surgery.

"You look fairly blooming this morning, Sally." Huw squeezed her arm in greeting, his nice face lighting up as usual at the sight of her as she stood busily filling her dressings trolley.

"Hello, Huw — it's the heat of rushing about this morning," she replied with a smile. Actually, he wasn't the first person to comment on her looks that morning. Myfanwy had insinuated that the previous evening she'd looked like 'a girl that had been thoroughly — well and truly kissed'.

Remembering deepened the colour in her soft cheeks and made her fingers tremble clumsily.

"Some days, I swear I do more stitching than a, dressmaker, Huw. Especially on Monday mornings."

He chuckled, glancing at her notes.

"You know why, don't you? Rugger and beer on Saturdays; booze again all day Sunday while the missus goes off to chapel. Not all of them mind, Sally, but it does explain the rush of cuts and so on on Mondays. Sharp metals, machinery and sore heads don't mix!"

Gradually they worked through the morning's surgery, breaking at last for a welcome cup of coffee.

"I'm doing some house calls this afternoon, Huw. Anyone special you want me to visit?"

"M'mm? Yes, old Tudor Jenkins — he's home after a bad ulcer op. Just check on him, *cariad*. And that one . . . and that . . . " he passed across the notes, and then leaned back looking intently at her face.

"And me, Sally — what about a visit to my home again?"

She bit her lip, thinking of his surly housekeeper, and not really wanting to repeat that awful evening again. Seeing the doubt in her eyes, Huw put in hastily —

"Would you rather we had a meal out? How about our popping over to Usk — lovely old hotel there?"

"I — I'm expecting something to crop up just now, Huw — something I can't discuss with you yet — probably will do so later. Can I take a rain-check for sometime later in the week?"

"Anything worrying you? You seem a bit distracted, Sally. Sure I can't help?"

"Not just yet, Huw." She reached out and patted his hand. "Bless you, I'll let you know."

Just at that moment, the door opened after the briefest of light raps and Richard Llewellyn stood there, taking in the cosy scene with a sardonic twist to his lips.

"Sorry, Sister — thought surgery was finished."

"It is. We're just having our coffee. Want some?" Sally's voice was cool, matching his. So it was back to Sister, was it?

"No thanks. Sorry to intrude, Huw. Just wanted to see Sister for a moment in my office."

With that he swung round and left them staring after his retreating back.

"Someone else with a load on his mind this morning! Well, Sally, I must be off. "Bye, love." Huw made no attempt to kiss her, for which she was incomprehensibly thankful.

Before going along to the PO's office, she tidied her hair, readjusted her pert little cap and powdered her nose. Like going into battle, she told herself with a grimace and straightening her shoulders as she tapped on the door.

"Come in. Ah — your doctor's gone, has he?"

"Yes, we've finished surgery." She sat down, her eyes anxiously scanning the strong face opposite.

"I've seen Alison Nicholls ... " he began and she felt a surge of relief flood over her.

"Oh thanks, Richard, How did it go — what did she say?"

Observing her eagerness, he leaned back in his swivel chair, stretching out his long legs.

"She said plenty — most of which I didn't like, but yes, I finally talked her into giving her promise not to have an illegal op. And to seeing you about going into a hostel for unmarried mothers later. She also said she'd accept help getting her baby adopted, but that's a hurdle to be met when the time comes, isn't it?"

"Richard ... I'm so glad."

"It wasn't easy. Fortunately she remembered that I'd been sympathetic when she applied for a job here and I took it from there."

She gave a sigh of relief, surprised at how tense she'd been, how anxious, wondering if he would succeed.

"Now — for the present, she can stay on here as long as possible," he went on.

"With time off for ante-natal care," Sally put in and he nodded.

"I'll leave that side to you. One thing I can do — we've a little two-desk office that deals exclusively with export and import documentation. The packers use a little hatch to pass through all the details needed — weights, sizes, etc. Alison will only need to show her head. It will get her away from the curious girls in the Accounts Department, I reckon. Also," he added, "I can arrange a bit of a rise in her salary — should come in useful and stop her worrying so much."

"Oh Richard, you're an angel," delighted, impulsively, she reached across to clutch his arm, only to feel his instant recoil. Embarrassed, she remembered the moment that morning when he'd caught her doing just the same to Huw!

"Sorry," she mumbled, "but I'm so

relieved." She rose to go as he replied —

"All part of my job, Sally." But they both knew it was more than that.

"Thanks again, anyway," and Sally was back in her own office before she remembered that she hadn't asked him anything about Megan's lorry driver . . .

6

LEAVING Megan in charge of the Medical Unit for the afternoon, Sally took her notes and a street map to begin her house calls.

Her cardiac case was expecting to go to the convalescent home and then back to a lighter job which Richard had found for him. He and his wife treated Sally like visiting royalty, insisting that she had saved his life and that they would be eternally grateful! He looked well and rested — a much better colour.

"I've packed up smoking, Sister and I'm down to one glass of ale a night now."

Pleased, she told him that, with care and healthier habits, and without stress, he'd live for years yet.

"Thanks to you, *cariad*," he echoed.

Her next call wasn't such a pleasant one. Stumbling through the rubble of an overgrown garden to the kitchen door, her heart sank. The signs of dirt and neglect were only too obvious, and the sight of the blowsy, slatternly woman who opened the door to her knock confirmed her fears.

"Oh — it's you," came the ungracious welcome. "Come by here . . . "

Her patient sat huddled over a smoking fire in the cinder-filled grate, and he looked terrible! Hiding her dismay and chatting cheerfully, Sally took his pulse and blood pressure and didn't like either! She inspected his almost healed wound and applied a fresh, light dressing.

"Stop your clothes from rubbing it for a day or two longer, m'mm?" His underwear was none too clean, but she pressed on, "How are you eating — the hospital dietitian gave you a list, didn't she?"

"He can't eat that stuff," the woman put in truculently.

"But he must — for quite a while yet," Sally insisted gently, and before she left she had their promise that he would stop living off the junk foods that made up their regular eating pattern.

Once he was back at work, Sally would

see that he ate a proper lunch, if nothing else. She sighed as she returned to her car; it was hard to tell people what to do in their own homes. In hospital, it was a different matter. Still, she'd done her best not to antagonize them, hadn't she?

She rang Megan from a call-box and hearing that there were no emergencies, made her way back to her digs.

"Two letters for you, Aunt Sally."

"Bless you, Ceri," she laughed at the young face upturned to hers, knowing just what was expected of her. "Jelly pastilles tonight — pet — for after tea, mind, or your mum'll skin me."

Chuckling, the little girl thanked her and went back to her TV programme, their nightly ritual over.

One letter was from her mother asking when she was coming home for another weekend, and the other was from Roz, her old room-mate at St Christine's . . .

' . . . our luscious Philip is letting it spread around (and you know just how things spread around *here*!) that *you* chased him unmercifully. His air of pathetic innocence is positively sickening. He's getting a lot of backing, too, from dear Mavis, the dragon's secretary. What a bitch she is! How's things going with your dishy Welsh doctor — do tell me more. I miss our little gossip sessions . . . '

As she read the scrawl, Sally could almost hear Roz's light voice, and suddenly she felt rather homesick for her friend and the familiar wards of St Christine's. She read the letter through again more slowly, and it hit her then that it had been ages since she'd thought of Philip. So much for that undying love, she mused sardonically in self-disgust.

"You can go to the Aberystwyth hostel about six weeks before your baby's due, Alison. Meanwhile, I want you to see your own doctor and the antenatal clinic regularly. You'll be given time off . . . " Sally paused looking across her desk to the young girl opposite. Was it her imagination, or was there a change in Alison? Her face looked softer, without its bitter, hard look; the surliness had left her mouth and her eyes were less wary.

"Now you know that you don't have to see this through alone. How do you like your new job?"

The slim shoulders shrugged carelessly.

"It's a bit quiet — I miss my pals."

"Of course you do, but later you'll be glad to be away from them a bit, won't you? This way you can stay on at work for ages yet," Sally told her. "Come and see me any time you like, won't you?"

"Thanks, Sister. I'm sorry I was a bit — er — off-hand when I came in before . . . "

"That's all right, Alison. I understand."

Sally made a note to keep an eye on the progress of the girl's pregnancy and wondered if she had time to scribble a note to Roz. Even as she reached for a sheet of notepaper, she heard someone come through outside, and she rose to see if she was needed.

"Not you again!" she exclaimed. "What is it this time — another cut?"

A grey face turned to hers and she almost gasped aloud. Never had she seen such wretchedness on a man's face before. His eyes were sunken deeply into their sockets, red-rimmed and bleary. His cheek bones stuck out prominently, and his hair was lank and uncared for. Mutely he held up a bleeding finger, and to Sally it seemed as if he was past caring whether it was bad or not!

"Sit down here." Gently she pushed him into a chair, pity welling up inside her. "Let's see, it's Jeff, isn't it? And this isn't the first time I've seen you lately, is it?" As she spoke she tended the deep cut on his index finger — it needed a suture to help it heal closely.

"I'm just going to have some coffee — care for some?"

He nodded numbly, and she told Megan —

"Plenty of sugar for Jeff, please."

As they drank it, she chattered quietly, waiting, hoping he would soon begin to tell her what was bothering him. It certainly looked as if the poor chap had come to the end of his tether.

"I — I must be going . . . " he half-rose to leave.

"No. No, stay a bit longer. They can manage without you, I'm sure."

He sank back gratefully into the chair and he looked so lost, her heart ached for him.

"Get on all right with your workmates, do you, Jeff?"

"Oh aye, it's not them . . . " he began and then stopped.

What is it then — you can tell me," she coaxed gently.

Suddenly, shockingly, the young man began to cry, great gulping sobs shaking his frame as the tears coursed unheeded down his face. For a second Sally sat rooted to her seat. She'd never ever seen a man cry like this before.

Then she hurried round the desk and instinctively reached out to cradle him in her arms. Like a lost child, he buried his head between her breasts, his tears soaking the front of her white uniform dress. Gently, as to a young child, she softly stroked his hair, holding him, rocking him as would a loving mother, her own eyes stinging with tears. God, she'd never seen a man in such a state — and such a young one at that!

Gradually, his sobs grew less violent, until at last, with a deep convulsive

169

sigh, he lifted his head and looked up shame-faced into hers.

"I'm sorry, Sister. Oh lord, I'm sorry . . . "

"That's all right, Jeff — possibly the best thing that could've happened to you."

She returned to her seat and waited, giving him more time to recover.

"Would do a lot of chaps good to have a weep now and then — like us females do."

He sat there slumped and spent and she knew she must find a way to help him.

"Now then, Jeff — feel like telling me all about it? And don't forget — it's for my ears only."

He looked down at his scarred hands, twisting them in his lap, as if he didn't know where to begin.

"It's my wife — she's left me. Gone off with another bloke."

Sally waited, something telling her that this wasn't the whole of the story. As if reading her mind, he shrugged.

"I wouldn't weep about that! She's no good — never has been. She's played around ever since our little girl was born."

As he said that, a spasm of sheer hellish pain passed over his face.

"No bloody good — ran me into debt — got me into trouble right and left, she did. Glad to see the back of her," he added and then paused.

"So . . . ?" Sally put in softly.

"She's taken my little lass with her, Sister. I love my kid with all my heart. She's everything that makes life worth while for me. And now she's gone, and it's breaking me up." He tightened his jaw, struggling to hold back his distress. "People think a man doesn't feel as much for his kids as their mother does, but it isn't so, Sister. That child's my whole life! I miss her so much . . . "

Sally swallowed against a lump in her throat — his sorrow was so obvious; he was utterly bereft without his child. She would have to help him.

"And you don't know where she is?" He shook his head.

"She — the missus — left a note saying she was going off with her latest fancy man, that's all, and I wasn't to try and find her because she was keeping Mandy."

Sally bit her lip, wondering where she could possibly begin . . .

"Look, Jeff, I want to help, but I might need to tell someone else — say the Personnel Officer for instance? You know Richard Llewellyn — he's a decent chap and what I tell him never goes any further."

As she spoke, she watched the shadow of doubt gradually leave his eyes, and he finally nodded his willingness to let her discuss it all with Richard.

"In the meantime, you'll have to pull yourself together, Jeff. You look a mess — and if you go on like this, you'll be killing yourself at your machine. And where will Mandy be then?"

She hated laying the law down, but it was for his own good.

"Have you anyone who will cook for you?"

With an effort, he brought his attention round to what she was asking.

"Aye — Mum'll do for me . . . "

"Good. So tonight — you go home, clean yourself up and get a good night's sleep. And tomorrow we'll see what we can do, m'mm?"

He rose, standing taller, looking better now that his burden was shared.

"Thanks, Sister, I'll do that. Thanks."

After he'd gone, Sally sat at her desk, deep in thought. It looked as if she'd have to consult Richard on this business too, and it occurred to her that they were working closer together lately.

Could it be that he was losing his earlier antagonism for her? Funny, but she found it so much easier to discuss her problems with him than with Huw, even though the doctor was such a kindly, caring man. But his involvement with the works was only minimal whereas Richard made it his whole life.

That train of thoughts led to another . . . surely such a virile, good-looking man had a woman in his life somewhere? It was a theory she hastily dismissed. It was none of her business, she told herself sternly, yet she was conscious of a feeling of desolation in the pit of her stomach.

"Here you are, Sally — notice for you of a working lunch on Thursday. They have them now and again for the managerial staff, that is." Sally looked up as Megan passed her the inter-office memo.

"Make a note in the diary, Megan love, in case I forget. How's things with you?"

She longed to warn her assistant of the forthcoming revealing of her boy-friend's little fiddle, but she knew she couldn't! As she signed the drugs' requisition list, she felt wretchedly guilty, but what could she do?

Two days later, she agreed to go out with Huw for a meal, knowing she would soon be baby-sitting for Myfanwy and unable to do so then.

"A good place for a meal is Usk," he told her as they started out. "There's several *cordon bleu* hotels as well as a super Italian restaurant — a lot of us locals drive over there for a decent meal."

Sally leaned back in her seat, at ease, letting the cadence of Huw's lilting Welsh voice wash over her — happy to be with this easy-going, pleasant man. No conflict, no arguments here, and right then Sally was thankful just to relax in his company.

He parked the car, suggesting —

"We'll have a drink at the bar first, eh Sally? Give us time to scan the menu."

She smiled back at him — he loved his food and was probably glad to get away from the dour Anna, too.

She raised her glass to his.

"Cheers, Huw," and as she did so she stiffened with shock. Through the pink-shaded mirror behind the bar, she caught the reflection of someone she knew!

"Oh, no!" She didn't realize she'd groaned aloud, and as Huw looked at her, she nodded and he, too, saw the image of Richard Llewellyn who was standing behind them, a beautiful girl by his side. They were so deeply engrossed in each other that Sally had time to look at his companion closely. Tall, as slender as a reed, the girl's long blonde hair shone in the light from the heavy old chandelier above. Her dress was daringly cut; her jewellery so obviously real, and her smile for Richard was intimate and inviting. Sally hated her on sight!

The force and depth of that hate shook her, and she had to put down her glass before it spilled over.

Puzzled, Huw murmured —

"Well, I did say Usk was popular for a night-out, and this is the best hotel. Do you want to go somewhere else — that is if you don't want to join up with them?"

How stupid to feel so shaken, just because Richard was out with a fabulous blonde. What on earth must Huw be thinking? All the same, she agreed —

"I'd rather we ate just we two . . . " she told him, and then felt guilty at the sight of the happiness that her words brought to his honest face.

"Me, too. Come on — we'll, try the Italian place. Signor Pergelli's an old friend."

Leaving the car, they strolled across the quiet old square and walked, it seemed, straight into the Bay of Naples; to be greeted fulsomely by the swarthy restaurateur. To candlelight, to soft Neapolitan music, they dined Italian style, with full-bodied wines and all the warmth of sunnier climes.

And Sally decided she liked having her hand kissed, being given a red rose to pin on her shoulder and being serenaded by a dark-haired, dark-skinned gypsy. During the evening, several people who knew Huw came over to chat, and she realized that a doctor had very little personal privacy; that she must never do anything to spoil his image. Not for Huw the freedom of the lovely day like the one spent with Richard.

And at the recollection of the PO with the beautiful girl, a little of the warmth suddenly left her.

It was perhaps unfortunate that the doctor chose that moment to propose! He reached across to clasp her hand, and he'd cleared his throat several times before Sally realized that he was about to say something important!

"We — we get on well together, don't we, Sally — we like a lot of the same things? We could work together — nurse and doctor — man and wife," he paused and surprised, her fingers jerked beneath his. "Wait, Sally, hear me out, *cariad*. I'm asking you to marry me . . . "

"Oh, Huw, darling . . . " Sally's feelings were in a turmoil; she felt flattered and honoured by his proposal, but — did she love him enough to join her life with his — for always? For her, marriage was meant to be forever.

"Think about it, my dear. You don't have to give me an answer right now. But you've come to mean such a lot to me, Sally, and I'd be good to you."

But at the idea of sharing that gloomy house of his; of living with the disapproving Anna, a gurgle of almost-hysteria welled up in her throat. And yet she knew Huw *would* be good for her, and that together they could have a fine life.

"I'll think about it, Huw. And thank you, darling, for asking me."

She bit her lip — it sounded so formal, "Bless you, love," she added, and she lifted his hand and pressed it to her soft cheek.

And the goodnight kiss she gave him at the front door was deeper than usual, for she was grateful that he hadn't pressed her for an immediate answer.

Myfanwy was in the kitchen knitting a jumper for Ceri; she looked up as Sally came through.

"Been kissed again?" she teased, refraining from adding that Sally didn't glow quite so much tonight! "Want some coffee?"

"No, thanks, I'm too full," and for a few minutes they chatted about her night out. "You must go there with your Terry, pet."

"Won't be long now. Oh, I'll be so glad to see him." There was a wealth of longing in the Welsh girl's voice, and just for a moment Sally envied her — at least *she* knew where her heart lay, didn't she? Briefly, she regretted Huw's proposal; they were such good friends — would it all be spoiled now?

Later, the thoughts scurried round her brain, refusing to let her get to sleep. She would have to see Richard in the morning to ask his help with Jeff's problem, but she wouldn't mention seeing him tonight, she told herself firmly.

One of her first patients the next morning was the canteen manageress, the garrulous Gwyneth Harris, with a nasty cut on her thumb. Tying off the dressing, Sally said casually,

"You'll have to stay away from food, Mrs Harris; but then, I'm sure you know the catering rules — no bandages, etc."

The other woman bristled, ready to do battle.

"But how'll they manage . . . ?" she snorted.

"You'll be there to supervise — tell them what to do, but no handling things yourself or we'll be in trouble with the Health Department. Sorry."

"M'mm, pity they haven't got more to do," and the look she gave Sally included *her* too!

As she slammed out, Richard Llewellyn passed her in the doorway. Seeing Sally's rueful glance, he murmured:

"Can't stand that woman. Can I see you before sick parade, Sally?"

"Yes, and I wanted to see you, too."

"Right." He sprawled comfortably in the chair opposite her suggesting, "Ladies first — fire away . . . "

Taking a deep breath to still the rapid heartbeats his presence always created, she began — slowly at first, then more desperately as the memory of a man's tears came back to her.

"What can we do for Jeff? Oh, Richard, if you could have seen him. Poor chap, he just had to let it all out."

He nodded pensively,

"I've seen how rotten he's been looking lately; too many minor accidents as well."

So he had noticed those, too? And once more Sally realized that there wasn't much he missed around there!

"Well now — firstly we must try and locate his wife's whereabouts."

"But how?"

"I've got my contacts. Actually, there's a retired police detective in town — does a bit of work now and again for the firm. I'll get him on to it. Shouldn't be too difficult to find her; folks don't miss much round here."

She answered his grin with one of her own at this Welsh character trait!

"And when you've found her?" she queried.

"That's up to Jeff. I suppose he'll be suing for a divorce; in which case he can ask for custody of the child. If what he tells you is true, he'll have no difficulty in getting either. It'll be just a question of time, and that's where you come in, Sally."

"What do you mean?"

"You'll have to keep talking him into a sensible frame of mind; see that he doesn't go off half-cock and spoil his chances — be patient."

"That won't be easy," she murmured doubtfully.

"We'll work together, don't worry. Besides, there's always a chance the wife's lover will get tired of having another man's kid around and Jeff'll get Mandy back before the divorce."

Happiness flooded through her then at his first sentence — all she wanted was to work alongside this man in harmony.

"Now — you wanted to see me about something?"

"Yes, Sally, it's about that scrap metal fiddle. The police have now got it in hand and they'll be arresting the culprits any time soon."

"Poor Megan . . . "

"And that's what I wanted to see you about. She mustn't know — she'll blow the gaff for sure. So, keep quiet to her, yes?"

"Of course. All the same, I feel sorry for her."

"She's young, she'll get over it. Just

infatuation probably." There was a wealth of scorn in his voice that made Sally protest.

"Your opinion of women is abysmal, Richard," and then even as she spoke, she remembered that once he'd told her how he'd been jilted almost at the altar. His dark eyes were watching her face intently.

"Oh, I don't know, Sally. My opinion of *one* woman's undergoing a change, I reckon."

And he rose to go, leaving her wondering if he was referring to his blonde companion of the night before?

Next day, the managerial luncheon was an absolute disaster ... Sally discovered it was to be held in the huge, oak-panelled board room, and to her surprise she saw that the long table had been covered by a decidedly crumpled, soiled-looking tablecloth. The place settings were haphazardly set; there were insufficient glass water jugs and no cruets!

With a hard glance down the length of the table, the managing director sat down in his chair at the head of it. The soup was cold, sloppily served by an obviously inexperienced waitress. When she made her next appearance with a congealing main course, her eyes were red-rimmed and she was hiccoughing her stifled sobs.

Angrily, the managing director turned to Richard at his side.

"Go out there and see what's happening, Richard. Tell Mrs Harris I want to see her — now."

Grim-faced, the PO rose to do his bidding and a few minutes later came back with Gwyneth Harris. One look at her smirking face made Sally's toes curl with apprehension. Smarming, the cook leaned over to listen to her boss's complaints, and then straightening up to her full height, she pointed dramatically down the table to where Sally was sitting.

"*She* told me, sir, not to go near anything. And all because of this little cut on my thumb! The girls can't cope alone, sir, but it's not my fault. *She's* always interfering . . . "

"That will do, Mrs Harris."

It was a stern-faced Richard who

dismissed her, but Sally could feel the displeasure of the whole table centred upon herself. It was all too clear what had happened. The canteen manageress had done this deliberately to make things look bad for Sally.

Anger blazed inside her then — she just wouldn't stand for being treated like this! Quietly she rose to her feet, and in a clear voice addressed the head of the table.

"When I treated her cut earlier this morning, sir, I reminded Mrs Harris of the Catering Hygiene code — no handling of foodstuffs whilst wearing a dressing, etcetera. I assured her it was still quite all right for her to supervise and so, sir, judging by the smoothly-running Works canteen I saw just now — all this," she threw her arm wide in disgust, "is quite unnecessary."

She sat down, her face burning, her soft mouth trembling as much with anger as dismay. Richard leaned over and quietly told his boss of the spitefulness and trouble he had with an otherwise good cook, and that the new Sister hadn't got used to her ways!

As Sally was about to protest, she caught the forbidding look in Richard's glance and snapped her lips tight on the words.

"Right — deal with it, Richard. See that it doesn't happen again."

Fresh meat and vegetables were served quickly after that, with a sweet and cheese board to follow. Over coffee the business of the lunch got under way, but much of it passed over Sally's head; she was still seething from the effect of the ugly scene earlier.

Her ears pricked up however when the managing director asked Richard how he and Sister Wakefield were working out?

"Fine, sir. We're working together on several cases at the moment. I think Sister is settling down very well." He turned his dark head and added. "What do you say, Sally?"

"Things are fine, sir, thank you," she agreed quietly. Later as she walked back to the Medical Unit, she found Richard at her side, and her anger boiled over.

"You — you didn't have to make excuses for me. Mrs Harris was in the wrong, not I," she exploded.

"I know. I'm sorry, Sally. I'll see to her, don't you worry. But I had to smooth things down as quickly as possible in there — that's another part of my job."

There was just the hint of a rueful plea in his voice, and Sally looked up at him quizzically.

"Sorry, Richard, but that woman gets up my nose." He stopped and turned towards her, and holding her by the shoulders, smiled down into her flushed face, his eyes darkly glittering.

"I know, *cariad*, I know. But don't let her — she's not worth troubling yourself about."

For a moment they stood there — close together, and the warmth of his hands on her shoulders made the pulse in her throat beat a rapid tattoo. From beneath her thick lashes, she looked up into his face and suddenly wondered what it would be like to be held in this man's arms . . .

The next day, everything seemed to be happening at once. Her landlady's Terry was due home that day, and they had spent ages the night before giving Myfanwy a complete beauty treatment. She certainly looked much better — slimmer, smarter, with shining hair and clear skin. Gone was the disconsolate droop to her mouth, and her eyes shone with happy anticipation as she saw Sally off to work that morning.

But when she entered the Medical Unit a different face greeted her. Poor Megan, her eyes were red-rimmed and swollen.

"They've taken him — caught him, red-handed. Oh, Sally, I should've known he was on to some kind of fiddle! All the money he spent on me; I'm to blame as much as him really . . . "

On and on she went and Sally tried her best to console her but in vain. Megan would be no good in the surgery like this.

"What'll become of him?" she wailed over and over.

"Get a suspended sentence and a heavy fine, I suppose. Of course, he'll lose his job here, but honestly, Megan, I shouldn't weep for him. By what I've heard, he's a bad lot. He could bring you down with him too. Try to forget him, pet. I know it's not easy."

She held the weeping girl close, trying to sooth away her tears. It was then that she had an idea . . .

"I want you to do some house calls for me, Megan. Remember the young chap, Mike, with the head wound — the one that got coshed in the loo?" Thankful to have caught Megan's attention, she went on, "Well, he's laid up with a bad dose of 'flu. I'd like to know if he's all right. And then there's these . . . "

Sally sighed with relief as she watched the girl's retreating figure; at least she couldn't weep all round the town!

"Taken it badly, has she?" Richard asked a few minutes later. "I wish we could have softened the blow; she's better off without that one — he's a born crook, I reckon."

"Meanwhile, I've got to work with her. She'll miss the nights out with him, too."

As he stood there, a pensive look on his face, she asked —

"Did you want something?"

"No — er — I just wondered . . . would you and Megan like to come to my place — say for a meal one night? My housekeeper's a good cook and it might help Megan take her mind off things a little."

Surprised, Sally thanked him and said she'd ask Megan and let him know. She hoped her young nurse would agree; she knew she was longing to see where Richard lived herself.

"I'm seeing Jeff this afternoon, Sally, and I want you to sit in on the talk, if you will?"

"Right — see you then . . . "

She had to hurry to get ready for the doctor's surgery and as she did, she realized she'd hardly had time to think about Huw's proposal. That fact alone showed her how reluctant she was to give him an answer.

Dear Huw — his face lit up as he bustled in to begin the session.

"Hello, darling, it's good to see you," and his eyes watched her face hopefully, expectantly.

"Huw — I've been so busy," she began regretfully.

"That's all right, Sally." His voice sounded partially relieved; had he been half-expecting her refusal?

With the onset of winter, there seemed to be more chest troubles than usual and as Huw put down his stethoscope for the last time, he shook his head, almost in despair.

"If only I could get more of these chaps to give up smoking, Sally! Three packets a day some of them." And what happens — every cold they get has a ninety per cent chance of developing into pneumonia or pleurisy."

Sally agreed with every word and wished there was more she could do.

"I'll put up some fresh posters, Huw — on the shop floors, washrooms and so on. If only Mrs Harris would let me make the canteen a non-smoking area."

But right then, the last person she wanted to tangle with again was the belligerent Gwyneth Harris!

"When am I going to see you again?" Huw began and she quickly interrupted.

"I've promised to baby-sit some nights for my landlady, Huw. Sorry."

Even as she spoke, she knew though that one date she wanted to keep was the meal at Richard's place, and she knew that even the excuse of lots to discuss was just that . . . a cover for curiosity and interest. Megan came back just before lunch, having completed her round of house calls. Going through the notes with Sally, her voice grew kinder as she came to those of the young man, Mike.

"He's still looking a bit groggy. The 'flu's really got him down, but his mum's a sensible woman. He — he's rather dishy, isn't he, Sally?"

"In spite of 'flu?" Sally laughed, eyebrows raised. Megan's cheeks grew pink.

"You know what I mean . . . " she protested and Sally agreed, glad to see the young nurse's thoughts veering away from her lorry driver!

"Oh, by the way, Megan, Richard Llewellyn wants you and I to have a meal with him one night — at his place. How about it?"

Megan's round face showed her surprise, her eyes wide.

"M'mm, yes, please, Sally. I wonder why . . . ?"

"Just a friendly gesture — towards you

mainly, Megan, that's all," and with that she told her to go for first lunch.

At three o'clock promptly, she went along to Richard's office to find he and Jeff already there, chatting.

"Sit down, Sally, we want you to hear all this seeing that you referred Jeff to me . . . "

Slowly, carefully the PO began to outline his plans to help. The ex-detective had already been given his instructions, and Richard had high hopes of his tracing the errant Mrs Richards and Mandy.

"But how long . . . ?" Jeff burst in desperately.

"As long as it takes, Jeff," Richard told him firmly, "unless you've a better suggestion?" The young man opposite shook his head mournfully, and Richard's voice softened as he went on —

"I know it's rotten for you, but you *must* be patient, Jeff. See this chap about starting divorce proceedings; I've already put him in the picture. Play it cool — get it settled properly and for good." He passed across a slip of paper, and then turned to Sally.

"Anything to add?"

"Well, I think Jeff should shut the house and go to stay at his parents' — let his mother take care of him for a while; pull himself together, or he'll end up losing his job," she said bluntly, but her eyes were full of sympathy. "Besides, Jeff, there's always the chance you might get Mandy back before the divorce."

He nodded his agreement and rose to go.

"I must get back. Thanks, both of you. It's good not to feel so alone," and with a nod to each of them, he left.

The PO sighed deeply.

"One of our long-running problems, that'll be, Sally, I'm afraid."

"Quite, but we'll both keep an eye on him though." "Oh, by the way, Megan says thanks for the invite — me, too."

"How about this Sunday then?"

Remembering that Myfanwy and Terry and Ceri were all going to visit his folks on Sunday, she agreed.

"Fine — shall I pick you up, or . . . ?"

"No, I'll collect Megan and drive us both over."

After Richard had given her clear

instructions how to reach his place, she left his office.

The nights were drawing in and soon it would be dark by going home time, she mused. It was as she and Megan were clearing up the surgery, completing notes and refilling for the next day, that they heard a loud noise — a tremendous clashing crunch of metals.

Thinking of the many lifts shunting heavy stuff around, Sally tensed, every instinct alert. A couple of minutes later, a white-faced Dai Jones burst into the office.

"Quick, Sally, Megan — bring all the first-aid kit you can carry. Oh God, there's been such a smash . . . "

7

AFTER that first brief moment of shocked silence, Sally recovered her wits and all her training stood her in good stead. Rapidly issuing orders to Megan, she began adding to the emergency bag.

"You've phoned for ambulances, police, Dai? Get Richard. We'll need lights out there, stretchers, blankets. Call Doctor Thomas, get Idris Williams, the first-aider. Megan, put on your cape and come with me . . . "

Lugging their supplies of extra bandages, dressings and pain-killers, they hurried from the Medical Unit and across the yard.

Long afterwards, Sally was to remember in her nightmares the sight that first met her eyes that cold, dark evening! A huge juggernaut, loaded with heavy packing cases, had hit the works' employees' bus head on, and even as they ran they could hear the cries and moans of those trapped

196

in the concertina'd coach.

A few — such a few — were struggling to climb out of the wreckage; staggering dazedly away from that hell pit. Within a few minutes — ages it seemed to Sally — lights were produced and she and Megan, together with Richard and Dai worked desperately trying to release more of the trapped workers.

Shortly afterwards she found Huw at her side, rapidly barking out instructions, trying to sort out and treat the more serious cases. Sally's heart was heavy as she slaved away under his commands. So many needed emergency treatment before they could be moved, and they worked hurriedly trying to give aid and succour to them all at the same time. There was so much to do . . .

"Coach driver's dead, Sally, and the chap sitting behind him! God — what a mess! Here's the ambulances — get that lot off first, love," and he pointed to the row of still figures on the grass verge.

The injured were lying all over the road, but many — too many — were still trapped amidst the broken seats and crushed metal within the wreckage.

Firemen and police, their faces dirt-streaked and sweating in the fitful light, laboured doggedly to release them, while Sally and Huw endeavoured to staunch as much bleeding as they could, in some cases setting up drips on the spot, and administering shots of morphia to the most badly injured.

"Huw — there's someone," that was Richard's voice, "a girl, I think, trapped by her legs. They're trying to move whatever's pinning her down, but she's in great pain . . . "

"Come with me, Sally . . . " Huw ordered briefly.

But try as he would, he couldn't reach the helpless victim. Guided by her moans, they cleared away as much debris as possible until a fireman told them —

"That's all. If we're not careful the lot'll cave in and kill her . . . "

"I can't reach her — not enough room," gasping Huw turned a dirt-and-blood-streaked face to Sally.

"Let me try, Huw. Give me the syringe and swabs."

Gingerly, Sally clambered up the tilted

side of the coach. Dear heavens, there was only a few inches between the tangled debris, and as she wriggled down, she felt the edges of heavy steel rip at her clothes, her arms and legs.

Even as she tried to move, the wreck groaned and creaked around her. There was blood — too much blood — and the hoarse, ugly moan of a human being in the depths of great pain.

Then thankfully, she could see a shoulder, arm and neck of the badly trapped girl.

"I'm coming, love. Can you hear me? Try and put your arm towards me if you can. It's Sister Wakefield and I can help you. Can you hear me?" Sally called louder this time.

There was still so much noise, dark and dust and cries from the injured that she could hardly make herself heard. Then, to her relief, there was an answering croak, a sound of a struggle and gasps of pain, but blessedly an arm was released and came inching through to where Sally could reach it. It took precious seconds to hack away some sleeve before she could finally administer the shot of morphia.

"Lie still, love. They're going to get you out any minute now. Lie still — I won't leave you . . . "

Quietly, Sally soothed the injured girl, and the answering groans grew quieter as the drug took effect.

At last, she was free to move, to struggle and inch her way back out of that cramped space. As she slithered down to the ground, every part of her hurt, and her legs, cut off so long from circulation, suddenly gave way and she felt herself falling . . . falling . . .

"Look out, she's fainting!" she heard a hoarse cry and then strong arms were lifting her — carrying her away from that awful carnage. Her cap, held by a last pin, hung over a strong arm, her tights had been torn to shreds as she'd crawled in and out of the smashed coach; her knees were bleeding from kneeling on the roadside gravel, and her dress was streaked with dirt and blood.

As she felt herself being lowered on to the examination couch in the surgery, she opened her eyes to see a white-faced Richard bending over her, his eyes bleak with anxiety.

"Oh Sally, my darling, I thought . . . "
He swallowed convulsively and grasped
her hands in his. "He shouldn't have
sent you in there — you could have
been killed . . . "

She struggled to sit upright, but he
gently pushed her down again.

"But I must get out there, Richard."

"They'll manage now — more help's
arrived and the last injured are being
ferried to hospital. Huw's going down
there to give them a hand — they'll
need it. And I'm going to see to these
cuts . . . "

He stood looking down at her, and his
face held a look that made Sally's heart
turn over in her breast.

"Sally, my love, you were marvellous
out there tonight," and he lifted her chin
tenderly, dirt and all, to kiss her gently
on her trembling mouth.

Carefully, he bathed the cuts and
grazes on her arms and legs. None
fortunately, were very deep, but they
certainly looked a mess! But as Richard
bathed and swabbed them, she thought
light-headedly, that it had been worth
getting them just to have him caring

for her so tenderly, to hear him call her 'darling'!

As he carefully applied the final dressing, she looked up into his face, longing to reach up and touch him, with a longing she could hardly deny.

"It isn't so difficult — to like me a little, is it, Richard?"

He tensed, standing there, still and drawn.

"Difficult?" The word came thickly from his hoarse throat. "The difficulty is trying not to take you in my arms — to hold you close — to . . . "

"Then why?" she whispered, all the hurt and bewilderment showing in her tired hazel eyes.

"Because, my dear Sally, there stands too much between us." He put down the bowl and before she could say anything else, he turned to go, saying —

"They'll be needing me out there — relatives to contact and so on . . . " and then he was gone, leaving Sally crying weak tears of shock and unhappiness.

It was late by the time Sally finally got to her digs. She had taken Megan home first. Her young assistant, too, was covered in scratches and dirt, and although she looked very tired, Sally noticed a tinge of quiet self-confidence in her eyes.

"You did well tonight, young Megan, as well as any old-timer . . . " And the girl in the car seat beside her stirred and gave a convulsive shudder.

"It was awful out there, Sally — so many hurt — and the blood . . . " She passed a shaking hand over her face, and Sally reached out to touch her sympathetically.

"Take a hot bath and get straight to bed, love. Try to forget it — for tonight anyway."

As the car drew up before Megan's home, Sally reminded her, hopefully to take her mind off the evening's tragedy —

"I'll pick you up Sunday to go to Richard's. OK? And thanks again, Megan, you're a fine nurse . . . "

Between them, in that little car, there was a mutual feeling of comradeship, of work well done, of complete understanding.

"'Night, love. See you Sunday."

Dismay shook her later as Myfanwy introduced her to Terry. Lord! what must he be thinking of her, looking like this? For an instant, Myfanwy thought her lodger had been in a crash herself.

"Oh Sally, you look awful — your poor arms."

Sally slumped wearily on to a kitchen chair, and quietly and as briefly as possible, told them what had happened.

"Anyone killed?" Terry asked sombrely.

"The coach driver and one other man. I — I don't know their names."

Reaction was setting in, and biting her lip to stop its trembling, she got up from the chair.

"I'll have a bath and go to bed, Myfanwy. Nice to meet you at last, Terry," she smiled wanly across at the stocky young man. He had a very attractive face; it was easy to see why Myfanwy was so much in love with him. "Don't forget I'll baby-sit tomorrow night," and with that she staggered up to her room.

Try as she may, she found sleep impossible. Her thoughts whirled in a turmoil inside her aching head.

What had Richard meant by 'so much stands between us'? Was he in love with the beautiful blonde? And yet tonight Sally could have sworn she glimpsed something in his eyes — something special — that had set up an answering echo in her own heart!

Lately, she thought he had lost some of that early antagonism — had grown to like and respect her and her work. But she must be wrong, and the thought made her heart feel like it was split in two. She pummelled her pillow and tried to settle to sleep, but she had so much on her mind.

Huw had worked like two men tonight; she had yet to give him an answer to his proposal. She knew they could have a good life together; both with the same caring interest in their work. He would always look after her, of that she was certain, but something held her back. Could it be that her experience with Philip was really stopping her from trusting another man? She was very fond of Huw, but was that enough? Would it be fair to marry him knowing that fondness was all she had to give him?

Suddenly as she lay there, she told herself how trivial were her own troubles, when somewhere in the town tonight some wife, some children were mourning the loss of a husband and father! Finally she fell into a troubled sleep, bedevilled again by the cries of the injured, the sights of that horrible crash — to wake at day-break unrefreshed.

Breakfast that morning at Caradoc Terrace was a merry affair though. It did Sally's heart good to see how much prettier Myfanwy looked, and she noticed that Terry's eyes followed his wife's movements all the while as she served them with breakfast.

When Myfanwy and Ceri hurried out to the front door to pay the milkman, Terry turned quickly to her —

"I'd like to thank you, Sally, for helping Myfanwy . . . you know — about that awful business with that woman . . . " His face crimsoned, the words stumbling out awkwardly.

"Glad I could help, Terry," Sally paused, and then went on, "Myfanwy's been working hard — on her figure, her hair, and so on. Please, just let her know you appreciate it — give her a good time this leave, m'mm?"

He nodded, but hadn't time to say more as his two females came bustling back into the kitchen.

"Daddy's brought me a Scottish boy dolly — with bagpipes an' everything."

"Come on and show me, pet."

And so Sally was able to take the chattering little girl off her mother's hands for most of the day. Up in the flat, she happily drew pictures while Sally replied at last to Roz's letter. She wondered whether to tell her old flat-mate about Huw's proposal, and then decided not to, and told her instead about her job and about last night's accident.

During the afternoon, she rang the local hospital to see how the casualties were faring. All seemed to be getting along all right, and saying she would visit them on Monday, she hung up, knowing the patients would have their own anxious relatives visiting them this weekend. Perhaps Richard could tell her more tomorrow, she mused, trying to ignore the rush of pleasure the thought of seeing him in his home produced.

She spent some time helping the happy Myfanwy get ready for her evening out. And she really did look good; the new dress made her look slimmer; her hair shone, and her make-up made her look so much more sophisticated, and the look in Terry's eyes boded well for the evening.

Sally played games with Ceri, read another chapter from their reading book, and when she had finally tucked the little girl into bed, decided to ring her parents.

"When are you coming home for a weekend, darling?" Her mother's voice held a plea that came over clearly.

"Soon, Mum — I'm still rather busy."

"Are you settling down all right, Sally? I do worry, you know."

And Sally knew she hadn't fooled her mother; her wise eyes had noted her daughter's unhappiness over Philip on her last visit home.

"I know, Mum darling, but you needn't. I'm quite over what had upset me. Yes, I'm settling in fine . . . " and Sally went on to tell her about Myfanwy,

Terry and Ceri and her pleasant digs; about Megan and Huw, and finally, about Richard.

It seemed to Sally that her mother was equipped with her own radar system, when she asked —

"He's the Personnel Officer, isn't he? The one you didn't like much — or was it that he didn't seem to like you? I forget which, dear."

Interrupting her mother's flow, Sally put in quickly —

"Oh, we get on fine now, don't worry, Mum. How's Dad keeping?"

Thankfully, she had managed to change the subject. Somehow she didn't want her mother asking too many questions about Richard; there were too many things puzzling Sally herself!

She washed her hair and treated her various abrasions; went to bed early with a new magazine and was asleep long before Myfanwy and Terry got home.

The following afternoon, she discarded one outfit after another, trying to decide what to wear. They were having drinks before an early evening meal and Sally wanted to look special — somehow different for Richard! Finally she chose a simply-made dress in a soft coffee-coloured jersey silk with its own little matching jacket. Her chestnut-brown hair gleamed with copper lights, and she had done her best to conceal the scratches on her face and arms. With the two-piece, she wore high-heeled, bronze kid shoes, with a little clutch bag to match. Her chunky gold ear-rings, a touch of perfume, and she was ready ...

"Gosh, you look super, Sally," Megan's greeting did a lot to raise Sally's spirits.

"So do you. We'll dazzle him tonight, eh Megan?"

The young nurse wore a trouser suit in a fine emerald-coloured wool, and for once her mane of black hair was dressed tidily around her typically Welsh face.

The outskirts of the town where Richard lived were new to Sally and she was glad of Megan's help to find it. She was surprised when they finally drew up outside a little old cottage. Not the rustic, thatched-roof type of her Midlands countryside, but old in the Celtic style. Made of huge stone blocks, square-set and sturdy, with blue slate-tiled roof, it had a pretty palisaded front garden overlooked by small-paned windows.

The door opened before they had time to use the gleaming brass door-knocker and Richard stood there to welcome them.

"You found it then? Can I take your coats?" Chatting happily, Megan didn't notice how his hands lingered on Sally's shoulders as he helped her off with her coat, or noticed how anxiously his eyes scanned the Sister's face.

"How are you both feeling — after the ordeal on Friday night?"

Having assured himself that neither had suffered any real ill-effects, he showed them into the little lounge. Sally fell in love with its old-world charm at first glance. Matt-white plastered walls and ceiling were interspersed by dark oak beams and panels. Matching Jacobean oak furniture was beautifully complemented by the heavy chintz covers and curtains. The armchairs and settee were deep and comfortable, with small tables easily to hand beside them. The books on the oak shelves looked well-used, and in the original old grate, a log fire burned brightly, highlighting the brass fire dogs and the polished boxseat fender.

Her satisfactory inspection completed, Sally gave a soft sigh of pleasure, and then realized that Richard had been watching her intently as she did so! He had already motioned Megan to a comfortable seat, and as he turned to Sally, he murmured —

"You like my cottage?" And if she hadn't known better, she would have thought her answer was important to him!

"Yes, I do," she breathed, "it's lovely . . . "

Just then a middle-aged woman came in with some more clean glasses, and her smile for the two visitors was wide and welcoming.

"This is Laura, my treasure and best friend."

With a deprecating glance in his direction, the housekeeper shook hands firmly.

"Nice to meet you, Sister. You, too,

Nurse. Richard's told me a lot about you both." Turning to her employer, she asked:

"Meal in half an hour?"

"M'mm, that'll be fine, Laura, thanks."

And Sally couldn't help but compare the amiable Laura with Anna, Huw's po-faced housekeeper — what a difference!

"Drinks, ladies?"

Sally asked for a Martini with ice and lemon, her favourite, but when it came to young Megan, her request was more complicated, so she jumped up and went across to help him sort it out. With much giggling on Megan's part and a look of sheer horror on Richard's, the young nurse returned to her seat bearing a tall glass which held a highly-coloured, extremely fizzy drink, duly decorated with fruit, ice and a cherry on a stick!

Watching Richard's patience as he pandered to Megan's whim, Sally leaned back in her chair and suddenly . . . as if she'd been hit by a flash of lightning she knew . . . She loved this man — with all her heart and soul! And would love him till the end of her days. That he would never return that love did not, at that moment, faze her. All she knew was that she loved him — not with a young girl's infatuation — not just 'in love' — but truly loving.

And she knew right then that there was a world of difference; that all she wanted was *his* happiness and well-being. Desolation at being unloved would come later she knew, but at that moment she just wanted to hide herself away in some quiet place; to take out and examine; to hug to herself — this precious knowledge. It was as if the light from a thousand chandeliers had replaced that from a penny candle!

Her face felt aflame, and through long lashes, she gazed down at her glass, holding it carefully with both hands so as not to spill her drink.

"Not to your liking, Sally?" Richard's soft query broke into her daydream, and she swallowed quickly before answering.

"No — er — yes, it's fine, thanks," and something in her voice made both the others glance at her flushed face.

"Lovely fire . . . " she held out a hand to the flames, hoping to excuse away her high colour!

Later they ate a deliciously cooked meal, with Laura making up a foursome. It was all too obvious that she adored Richard and as they ate, with that to-and-fro asking of leading questions so rife in Wales, it was soon disclosed that she and Megan's mother were girls at the same school! And as they chatted, Sally could hardly hold back a smile, it was always the same.

Still deep in reminiscences, Megan went through to the kitchen, insisting on helping with washing up the dishes. Or was she being tactful, Sally wondered?

"Heard from Huw since Friday night?" Richard on the other side of the fireplace sat with his long legs stretched out before him, relaxed in his casual hand-knitted sweater and corded jeans.

"No, he was probably on call." Something — possibly the revelation of her new-found love — made her suddenly blurt out —

"He — Huw's asked me to marry him."

His face half-turned away from the revealing light from the fire, Richard's voice was low and controlled.

"And what did you say? Jumped at the chance, I suppose?"

Sally bit her lip against a bitter retort, and shook her head slowly.

"I — I haven't given him my answer yet."

"Keeping him on tenterhooks, eh? Making him all the keener no doubt!"

Her hazel eyes glistening with threatening tears, Sally whispered —

"Oh Richard — why do you hate me so?" and the heartache in her voice almost unnerved the watchful man opposite.

Just then Megan came in from the kitchen, and Sally jumped up, mumbling —

"Excuse me . . . the bathroom . . . " and she dashed out of the room before she broke down and made a complete fool of herself.

When she returned, several minutes later, she knew that Richard and Megan had been talking seriously together, although apart from his first enquiry, all of them had deliberately not mentioned the crash. But it was on the way home, after listening to some records and drinking several cups of excellent coffee, that Megan told her —

"Richard told me — when you were in the loo — how he sorted out about the scrap metal fiddle. He was truly sorry that I'd had to be hurt in the process, but as he said, he had to do the right thing by the firm and so on. He was so kind — said you and he would help me get over it." She paused, looking out for a road sign, and then went on, "I told him how good you'd been; how you'd told me you knew what it was like to be in love with the wrong sort of chap! That's why you moved down here, I said."

Through a tight constriction in her throat, Sally asked —

"And what did he say to that?"

"He looked a bit, well — queer sort of, and asked me if I was sure — if that's really what you said?"

The young nurse turned in her seat, trying to see Sally's face in the dim interior of the car.

"D'you know, Sally, I reckon Richard Llewellyn's keen on you!"

"I'm sure he's not . . . " Sally put in quickly, wishing she could change the subject.

"Well, I've seen the way he looks at you — when you're not looking, I mean, and I think he really fancies you."

Sally gave a little laugh that didn't quite make it, and she was thankful when she finally dropped Megan outside her home.

"Don't be late in the morning, we've lots to do. 'Night."

But instead of going straight to Caradoc Terrace, Sally drove to a quiet spot way above the town which, in daylight, gave a beautiful view in each of the four directions.

Tonight it was cold and dark, but the sky was clear and full of brilliantly shining stars; from up there the lights of the town below seemed to be like twinkling jewels. Alone at last with her fantasies, she began to think of her life, and how being in love with Richard was going to affect it.

She knew now for certain that she couldn't marry Huw. It wouldn't be fair to him — knowing that she would always be longing for another man, always craving to be in another's arms. And being young, she wistfully dreamed of what it would be like to be loved by Richard — to know his kisses all the time, to have them set her on fire with their passion. She wondered, too, just how long she could go on working at Dustrax Limited alongside Richard — seeing him every day; wanting to touch him, to be more than just a colleague?

Quietly subdued, with a deep ache in her heart, she turned the car downhill, and not wanting Myfanwy's perceptive eyes to see her face just then, she simply called out a cheery "Goodnight" kitchenwards and went straight up to her room. And her pillow was damp with her tears long before she finally dropped off to sleep . . .

8

THERE were the usual Monday morning thick heads; the soiled dressings to be changed the next morning, and Sally was thankful it wasn't Huw's day for a surgery.

It was cowardly she knew, but she dreaded telling him of her decision, hated the thought of destroying the look of happiness on his nice face.

When she found herself repeating her queries over and over, she asked the oldish man in the chair in a loud voice —

"Are you having trouble with your ear, Bryn?"

"Eh? Me — no, Sister. It's you whispering; speak up, lassie."

Amused, Sally reached for her otoscope to examine the workman's ears, and as she suspected found them blocked by solidified wax and dirt. Trying to explain that he needed an application of oil to soften the wax before she finally syringed his ears clear was an exhausting business.

"Come and see me Wednesday, Bryn."

As he went out muttering to himself, she wondered ruefully if he would thank her — sometimes silence was bliss, especially on the noisy workshop floor!

"You're going to the hospital this afternoon, aren't you, Sally?" As she looked up at him from her notes, there were dark circles beneath her eyes and an unusual droop to her soft mouth.

"Yes, Richard. How about the relatives of those two men who were killed?"

"I saw them on Saturday — awful business." She could see by the tightening around his mouth how the visits had affected him. "Coach driver leaves a wife and two teenagers. The other man was older — a widower, who lived with his sister. I've promised all the help we can give . . . "

A silence hung between them for a moment, both busy with their thoughts, and then Sally sighed. She had known many such tragedies at St Christine's, but it never grew more easy to bear, but one had to go on..

"Thanks for the pleasant evening last

night, Richard. We both enjoyed it and I'm sure it did Megan good; helped her forget her troubles for a while."

"And you, Sally . . . ?" He leaned over and looked into her eyes. "Did it help you at all?"

She swallowed hard — had she given herself away? He must never know how much she loved him. But yes, last night had helped her to resolve her answer for Huw, hadn't it?

"I loved your cottage, Richard, and it was nice to renew my acquaintance with your corgi." Deliberately, she avoided the question in his eyes. "And you're lucky in your Laura — she's a smashing cook."

"Oh, Sister . . . " Thankful for the interruption — she was needed to remove a steel splinter from the streaming eye of the young man standing in the doorway, and Richard left.

She spent a busy afternoon at the hospital, both in the Men's and Women's wards. Some of the patients were more badly injured than others, but practically all of them were pleased to see her. Nevertheless, by the time she got home that evening, she felt drained and exhausted, and was thankful when young Ceri finally settled to sleep. The child was overexcited for Terry was apt to spoil her during the days of his leave, and childlike she responded with the odd stubborn tantrum.

Myfanwy looked as if she was on cloud nine, and had managed to whisper a few words to Sally when Terry was getting ready to go out.

"He says I — we can have another baby, Sally. I'm coming off the pill, and next leave . . . "

Her cheeks grew pinker, her eyes glowing like twin orbs of light, and Sally hugged her close, pleased that all was going so well with her young landlady.

"Good for you, Myfanwy, oh, I'm so glad."

"And what about you, Sally? I've noticed lately you . . . "

Sally turned aside and fiddling with a spoon on the draining-board, replied quietly —

"I'm OK, Myfanwy. Think I'll take a weekend home soon — when I'm through baby-sitting, that is," she added hastily. "Think I need a break."

But at the thought of not seeing Richard, of being miles away from him, her throat thickened, misery a solid lump inside her.

"You get off, Myfanwy. Have a good time; I'll put Ceri to bed, love."

And so now she was alone, with her thoughts. So much had happened these last few days . . .

Huw's greeting the next morning was as warm as ever and Sally hoped he didn't notice that she turned her cheek instead of her mouth to his quick little kiss.

He looked tired, and his normally jovial face had lost some of its colour.

"Busy weekend, Huw?" she asked sympathetically.

He nodded with a wry grimace.

"M'mm — one of the partners has got the 'flu, another on a few days refresher course, and you know what it's like with a locum? It seems that half the town's down with 'flu as well . . . "

"Poor Huw — that crash was hellish for you, too, love." And for a few moments they discussed it, and the prospects of those injured in hospital. Then he reached out and held her by the arms.

"You were marvellous, Sally," he looked into her face fondly, "We'll be a grand team."

Hurriedly she veered the conversation. "Are you free tomorrow night for a little while? Say — for a run out somewhere for a drink and a chat?"

"Yes, of course, darling . . . " Expectantly the doctor's eyes lit up, and afraid he was getting the wrong idea, Sally handed him the rota quickly —

"Here's today's list . . . "

She thought Megan looked more cheerful as she opened the Medical Unit the next morning, and she didn't have to wait long before the young girl confided,

"By the way, Sally, I've returned all the gifts — the jewellery and stuff to . . . " she paused and then went on, "I went out with Mike last night. He's great fun and we had a smashing time."

"Good for you, pet — I thought you looked a bit brighter," Sally replied, but she did wonder whether to warn Megan that Mike's motto was "love 'em and leave 'em" and then decided not to; perhaps he was just the right person to make her forget her recent heartache.

There was a long sick parade that morning, with quite a few more chest infections, and although Sally dropped several gentle hints about giving up smoking, she knew that, in most cases, she was wasting her breath!

Bryn Jones came in to have his ears flushed out, and when, after the second attempt, quite a good-sized wedge of hard wax floated out, he winced at the sudden in-rush of noise! After she'd done the other ear, he was bitterly complaining that he'd rather be a bit deaf, thank you, Sister, than hear all this row!

"Off you go, Bryn. Don't let your mates know you're hearing better — you'll be surprised what you'll overhear!"

He shook his grey head, a wide grin on his wrinkled face.

"You're a wicked lass — but lovely with it . . . "

She finished work early that evening, which gave Terry and Myfanwy time to go to an early performance of a local choir concert. Ceri was in bed by the time they got home, and Sally was ready to pop out to meet Huw.

The little country pub was almost empty as they took their drinks to a corner table; Huw had also ordered a plate of ham sandwiches for himself.

"Missed my meal tonight, Sally, and I'm famished."

Dear Huw, he did need a wife to care for him, and just for a moment Sally wondered if she'd made the wrong decision? But thinking of the years ahead — of loving another man, she knew she couldn't do that to him.

Passing her tongue nervously over dry lips, she reached across and caught Huw's hand tightly in hers.

"I've made up my mind, darling . . . " she began huskily, looking deep into his eyes, finding it so hard to go on.

"And it's No, isn't it, Sally? I can tell."

The regret and unhappiness in his voice filled her with remorse, but she had to go on —

"It wouldn't be fair to marry you — I don't love you enough, Huw, not in the right way. I'm very fond of you, yes — but it's not enough! I've made one mistake . . . " and quietly she told him all about Philip, and why she had taken the post in Wales, to make a fresh start.

"I didn't know he was married, Huw, honestly I didn't — none of us did."

He swore softly under his breath, concern for her masking his own disappointment for a moment.

"I'm sorry, Huw, you're such a grand person — I couldn't do that to you."

Tears sparkled in her eyes — she'd never felt so wretched!

"Is there someone else, Sally?"

Twisting the stem of her glass between nervous fingers, she couldn't quite meet his eyes as she shook her head.

"No one else that I shall be marrying . . . " she murmured, and if that didn't quite answer him, she was sorry, but she couldn't say more.

"Can we still be friends, Huw? I need your friendship so much," she pleaded softly.

"Of course, *cariad* — always," and his lips stretched into a smile that cut Sally to the quick.

During the following week, Sally felt as if she was under some dark cloud. She and Richard along with what seemed to be half the work force of Dustrax Limited attended the two funerals. It had always intrigued her how many friends, relatives and colleagues attended a funeral in this part. The chapel was overflowing, and the beautiful clear voices raised to the roof in the singing of the hymns.

She felt as if a slight rift had grown between her and the doctor in spite of his promise to remain her friend. Or was it just her own conscience bothering her? All the same, there was slight sense of strain in their formerly happy relationship.

Myfanwy and Ceri were also a bit down after Terry had gone back up north again.

Only Megan seemed brighter; she was having a good time with the exuberant Mike, and seemed to have completely recovered from the distress of having her lorry-driver boy-friend disgraced and dismissed.

Winter had well and truly set in, she thought ruefully, as she packed another woolly into her small suitcase. She had decided to go home from Friday night till Sunday, and little Ceri was watching her with anxious eyes.

"You *are* coming back, Aunt Sally, aren't you?"

Sally hugged her close, swinging the little girl high off her feet.

"Of course I am, pet. I'll be back again on Sunday. And you can look after Mummy for me, can't you?"

There was a white fringe of snow on top of the mountains as she turned her little car towards the Midlands motorway. She hadn't seen Richard all day, but Megan knew of her trip home and expected her back in good time for surgery Monday morning.

Somehow the dense lanes of traffic fouling-up the intertwined motorways near Birmingham seemed to bother her as never before; she'd grown used to the gentler, slower pace of life in the valleys! There, folks always seemed to have time for a good old gossip; time to care for their neighbours. Money and rank meant nothing at all to the folks down there. Only two things, she smiled to herself, rugger and choir practice;

both were sacrosanct to the sturdy Welsh-man!

She knew she would hate to leave her post at the works, but how could she stay on and see Richard every day — loving him as she did with all her heart? Knowing he didn't even like her? Perhaps seeing him again with the lovely blonde girl?

By the time she reached her parents' home, she was in need of their warm, loving greeting.

"Oh Sally, darling, we have missed you. You've lost weight!" her mother hugged and accused on the same breath.

"Not an ounce!" Sally declared, kissing her mother's soft cheek. "Hello Dad, you've not lost weight, that's for sure," and she reached out and patted his bay window fondly.

"Still as cheeky as ever," he growled, pleased to see this favourite daughter.

It was good to be home, to be fussed over and pampered, to be able to say what she liked, do what she wished!

She helped her mother with the dishes, idly gossiping as her father dozed in his chair in the lounge, telling her of some of the amusing things about her work.

"I hope you get out occasionally, too, darling. You know — all work and no play . . . "

And so Sally told her about Huw and their outings; his proposal and her refusal.

"But why, Sally? He sounds just right for you."

Sally, knowing how anxious her mother was that she married and gave her some longed-for grandchildren, shook her head sadly. Rubbing energetically at the dish with the tea-towel, she went on —

"I don't love him, Mother. Oh, he's nice and kind, a lovely man, but being fond is not really enough, is it?"

And she spoke with such heartfelt conviction that the older woman knew — her daughter loved someone else, and that love was a yardstick to measure by, wasn't it?

For a moment, as she fished around in the bottom of the suds for an elusive teaspoon, Mrs Wakefield prayed that things would turn out right for her beloved daughter! She deserved to be happy now that she was over whatever had driven her to go down to work in Wales.

As for Sally, she longed to throw herself into her mother's arms and tell her all about Richard, and the stupid, wasteful love she had for him! But both concealed their deepest thoughts, and when the time came for Sally to leave, she hugged her parents close, promising to be home again soon, to write often.

"Give us a ring, love, to say you're back safely." Dear Dad, he still thought of her as a little girl.

"Been home, have you?" Richard poked his head round her office door early the next morning, and to Sally it seemed ages since she'd seen him.

"Yes — saw my folks for the weekend."

"Only your folks?" Something in the question made her blink and stare up at him.

"Of course, why?"

But he shrugged and then went on —

"There's a message for you. Megan's down with 'flu; her mother's just phoned in. Can you manage . . . ?"

"Of course!" she told him tartly.

"Poor Megan that'll put paid to her social whirl for a few days."

"She's only young; she'll settle down eventually," Sally replied defensively. "She's a splendid nurse."

"Well, let me know if you need any assistance and I'll get in a 'temp'."

Knowing how short-handed the local hospital and doctors' units were, she muttered,

"You'll be lucky," rebelliously under her breath and began preparations for the first sick parade. She was rushed off her feet, but the men were all very patient and understanding, all trying to be as little trouble as possible.

However, it was Dai Jones who later brought in a white-faced workman, who was muttering over and over,

"I'll not let her near me, Dai, she's only a young lassie . . . "

"What's happened, Dai?"

The front of the man's clothing was all burnt and charred, and he was clutching his lower parts, obviously in great pain. Even as she spoke, Sally persuaded the man to lie on the couch. He was badly burned, but in no way was he allowing

Sister to tend his burns — his 'private parts' as he put it!

After all the time spent on the Men's Wards, she was quite used to this ridiculous show of modesty on the part of some of the older men.

"Phone for an ambulance, please. Dai — if I give you a dry dressing, can you please put it gently over the burn area? Fine — get your hands scrubbed," she ordered and turning to the man, asked gently, "Will that do, Bill, till you get to the hospital?"

He grunted his assent through clenched lips, and it wasn't long before the suffering man was whisked away to the hospital, with Sally asking why he hadn't been wearing protective clothing? Apparently, he'd been using an acetylene torch to cut metal and dropped it, with dire effects to his scantily protected 'private parts'.

"I guess this'll teach them all a lesson, eh Sister?" Dai Jones chuckled as he left the surgery.

Richard rang through as she toiled away.

"Checking up on me," she fumed silently.

"Just to let you know — I'll go to the hospital today, Sally."

Somewhat remorseful, she thanked him and replaced the phone, and set about clearing up the surgery before the next batch of patients.

The 'flu epidemic raged — no respecter of persons — for the next few weeks, and the cold, bleak weather didn't help. She had been out twice with a tired looking Huw, hoping to revert to the previous state of friendship between them. But now and then as they ate, she would look up to catch a wistful look in his brown eyes. He was still hoping to get her to change her mind, she knew, by the little things he dropped out from time to time. Like asking for her suggestions about doing up the house, choice of colours, and so on. And Sally felt uncomfortable and unhappy knowing that whatever he did, she would never be sharing that house with him!

Once she went out for a spin with Richard. He had complained that she was looking wan and needed a breath of fresh air, and Sally, too tired to argue, had agreed.

"I've got a schoolboys' rugger match to referee this afternoon, Sally," he announced as he picked her up from Caradoc Terrace.

He looked so handsome in his leather jacket and soft woollen sweater that she longed to throw herself into his arms and beg him to love her as she loved him! Instead, she took a deep breath and climbing into the front seat, told him calmly —

"That's fine, Richard, I've got some shopping to do myself before the shops close."

She watched his strong hands as they rested on the driving wheel; the pale sunlight revealing the dark hairs on the back of them. Was she being stupid to punish herself like this? Stupid being here beside him; but even as she asked herself the question, she knew she hadn't the strength of mind to refuse his invitation. Half a loaf was better than none when it came to unrequited love, she told herself sadly.

Swiftly, competently, he drove up and

out of the town, and then made gradually round the perimeter of a man-made reservoir, to one of the tiered car-parks on the other side. The area had been beautifully landscaped, creating a large, open picnic spot where cars were able to park for the best views.

Today the water looked cold and dark; the mountains and hills behind making a bare, natural backdrop.

"It's lovely here in the summer," Richard told her winding down his window to let in the sharp, cold air. "The water's covered then by colourful sailboards and fishing boats — plenty of room for everybody. Want to stretch your legs?"

"Please." And to avoid the touch of his hand beneath her elbow, she hurried on before him — across the tufted grass, over towards a stile and into the woods.

The dead, brown-coloured bracken crunched beneath their feet as they walked slowly side by side; the wind rustling the bare branches and lifting Sally's hair like a bronze-coloured veil.

"Popular with sweethearts this during the Summer," he told her with an impudent grin. "Round here the local lads boast of having 'a fern ticket' for tonight — meaning they're going to walk out with their girls that evening."

Unable to stop herself, Sally blurted out —

"Do you do that, Richard, with your blonde girl — have a fern ticket, I mean?"

He stopped in his tracks and turned to face her. There was an unfathomable look in his dark eyes and the corner of his mouth lifted quizzically as he gazed down into her face.

"Blonde girl . . . ?" His eyebrows were two black question marks.

I saw you with her — one night when Huw took me for a meal at that Italian place in Usk." Her hair hung like a curtain shielding her flushed face. What on earth had possessed her; letting him know that she'd been perturbed by the sight of him with another girl?

With one gentle brush of his hands, he pushed aside her hair, cupping her woeful face and tilting it up to his, to stand gazing down deeply into her eyes.

"Ah, the admirable doctor! And when

are we to expect the list round for your engagement present, Sally?"

"Never! No — I'm not going to marry Huw." As if mesmerized his eyes held hers, and only her last shred of pride stopped her from blurting out the truth — telling him that she couldn't possibly marry another man!

"Why, Sally?" Just two quiet words, but suddenly she felt it was important to him — that he really wanted to know.

"I — I don't love him — not enough to marry him — to spend the rest of my life . . . "

Through the touch of his hands on her cheeks, Sally felt a sort of tension drain out of him, and her answering glance held a hint of puzzlement.

"For life? That's a bit old-fashioned these days, isn't it?" he jeered. "You've missed a, good catch there, *cariad*. I thought you fancied him."

"I'm fond of Huw; he's a good person," she began.

" . . . but fond isn't enough, m'mm?" he finished for her, and then, dropping his hands he turned and they resumed their walk, both deep in thought.

At the far edge of the little wood, they turned back and retraced their steps to the stile. Once there, Richard reached out and taking her arm, pulled her close to his hard chest.

Sally felt the breath catch sharply in her throat, and even as she turned her head, her lips were claimed by his! Gently at first and then more fiercely demanding, they teased hers into response.

"I don't have a fern ticket, my darling, but I do have the girl . . . " The whispered words fanned her cheek and then his mouth descended again, and Sally found herself reaching up behind his head, to pull his lips closer and closer . . .

The yapping of his little corgi in the distance brought them both down to earth.

"Sorry, Sally, I shouldn't have done that . . . " he muttered, helping her over the stile.

"No — you shouldn't have," she told him heatedly, but deep down the anger was at herself for responding so fervently to his kisses.

She clenched her fingers tightly in her

palms, berating herself mournfully, "How could I? Where's my pride?"

Deliberately, she kept their desultory chat to commonplace things, hating herself for her momentary weakness; hating him for taking advantage of it!

Back outside her digs, she collected her handbag, hurrying to escape, but even as she scrambled out of the car door, he was there, standing tall, blocking her flight.

With one long finger, he raised her chin and placed a light butterfly kiss on her parted lips.

"'Bye, Sally, see you Monday," and he was gone.

"Damn you, Richard Llewellyn," she fumed and flounced up to the front door, seeing it through a haze of angry tears.

When Megan returned from sick leave, she was still a little hollow-eyed and wan. The 'flu epidemic was on the wane, and folks were beginning to look forward to Christmas. The shops in town were starting to fill their windows and counters with toys; to dig out last year's decorations; urging shoppers to buy early; to post early.

Like an excited child, Megan began telling Sally all about the huge Christmas party they had every year in the Works' Canteen.

"We all help, you'll see. And we have a great time — wives, husbands, children, sweethearts, everybody's invited!"

Sally was used to the excitement and preparation that went into Christmas on the wards, but this was something different entirely. All the female staff were engaged in designing and making the decorations and trimmings for the tree. The canteen girls were to be in charge of refreshments, while the shop floor men and all those on dirty jobs contributed cash for toys and presents.

Dai Jones was traditionally their Santa Claus, and a small fork lift truck was to be scrubbed and decorated as his trusty sleigh.

"This looks a bit worse for wear, Sister." Dai held up the huge red costume, just back from the cleaners. "Losing a bit of its fluff, I reckon."

"Give it to me, Dai, I'll soon fix it."

The Medical Unit was being raided every day for cotton wool, scissors and anything else the staff couldn't scrounge elsewhere! This year the children were being asked to come in fancy dress, and Ceri, who was to be Sally's guest, couldn't make up her mind what to wear.

"I wish I was grown-up and pretty like you, Sally."

"And sometimes I wish I was a little girl like you, Sally laughed, and then had an idea.

"I know, we'll swap places, Ceri — you go as Sister Wakefield!"

Eyes sparkling, the youngster clasped her hands gleefully, and so they began to make her outfit. Myfanwy unpicked an old white dress of Megan's and remade it smaller; Sally made her a miniature version of her own cap. Complete with toy stethoscope, thermometer and watch, her hair tucked up tight, and a smear of make-up on her chubby cheeks — and she looked just right!

"What are you wearing, Sally?" Myfanwy asked.

"I'm going to Cardiff and buy myself the loveliest frock I can find, and blow the expense!"

Refusing all offers of help and advice, she set off the last Saturday before the party. To her dismay, she found just about every other female in town had the same idea! The shops were crowded, sales girls short on temper, and she couldn't find a dress that really pleased her.

She had given up hope and was driving back slowly through a small village when her eye was caught by a tiny bow-windowed shop. Painted black and white, it was the most elegant little boutique she had seen that day. Only one or two items were displayed in the small window, so she decided to go inside and see what she could find.

The chic, middle-aged owner was decidedly helpful, and seemed to know exactly what Sally wanted. Ignoring the dress rails, she murmured —

"I have one lovely model — a client left a deposit and said she'd collect it a week ago, but I don't think I'll keep it any longer for her."

With that she went through a curtain into the back room and returned with *the* dress!

On the hanger it looked nothing out of the ordinary, but once on Sally's trim figure, it was a dream. Dark, midnight blue organza over a silk slip, it was picked out here and there with a gleam of silver. Beautifully draped, leaving one smooth shoulder bare, it was all Sally could desire. It was perfect!

"I'll take it," she breathed.

"But, madam, the price is . . . " The price was staggeringly high, but Sally felt reckless for once, and made out the cheque without wincing.

"I'll have to go back to Cardiff for some shoes."

When the shopkeeper came back with the dress in a box, she held out her hand.

"Would you like these ear-rings — as a gift from me? I bought them with this dress in mind."

Expensive-looking, long, in sculptured silver, they were just right for the dress.

"Oh, thank you . . . " Looking at her customer's delighted face, the woman beamed.

"My pleasure, my dear — have a lovely party."

"I will, thanks again. 'Bye."

Of course, she just had to put it on to show Myfanwy, but had enough sense not to mention the price.

"You look really beautiful, *cariad*, truly."

"Thanks, Myfanwy. Look, I brought this for you — an early Christmas prezzie."

'This' was a white silk blouse, wickedly demur, with rows of lace-edged pin-tucks and full-sleeved with tight cuffs. She knew Myfanwy already had a good long black skirt in silk jersey.

Happy tears gleamed in the Welsh girl's eyes.

"Bless you, Sally. Oh, I do love you . . . " and she hugged her close.

"Hey, don't crease your new blouse. How about a cup of coffee, pet?"

In spite of the excitement of the coming festivities, work at the Medical Unit went on as usual, with the everyday list of cuts and burns, migraines and pains; some injuries worse than others. Megan began to regain her old sparkle, helped Sally suspected, more than somewhat by the attentions of the good-looking Mike. But Megan had learned her lesson. This time she wasn't neglecting her studies; didn't let him keep her out late at night. In fact, she was playing it hard to get, and Mike was anxiously trying to put their relationship on a more permanent basis.

Just after the doctor's surgery had finished one morning shortly before Christmas, Richard was teasing the young nurse; getting back as good as he gave, and Sally, toying with her coffee, watched them wistfully, wishing she was in Megan's shoes right then, longing to recapture a closer rapport between herself and the PO.

And so she sat there, not knowing that her face revealed her longing to Huw seated on the other side of the desk. Suddenly he knew why Sally didn't love him enough to become his wife! Oh, it was clear now — she was in love with Richard Llewellyn. What a damned fool he'd been! Of course, he should have seen all the signs before . . .

And Richard — what did *he* feel for Sally? Somehow the doctor didn't think the younger man was entirely immune to her attractions! Sadly, forlornly, a heavy ache in his heart, he knew that, above all, he wanted Sally to be happy . . .

The afternoon of the party came round at last. The canteen had been transformed, and a huge Christmas tree, glittering with baubles and tinsel and fairy lights, stood in the corner. Long, trestle tables groaned under the weight of the food and drinks. Excited youngsters were bebopping to the disco at one end of the long room. Dads and mums gathered in groups; young ones and older ones, according to their ages and inclinations; chatting noisily, their lilting voices calling across to each other, renewing acquaintances, thoroughly enjoying a good party.

Sally, looking really beautiful in her lovely dress, was blushingly acknowledging the heavy-handed compliments from her ex-patients, meeting their wives and children.

It was as she was leaning over to admire a new baby in its carrycot on a chair beside a young mother, that it happened . . .

The proud father, a worker from

the extrusion department, was leaning forward, joining in the talk about the baby. He'd been about to light a cigarette, and had the lighter in his hand at the very moment a little girl danced by — her net ballet tu-tu whirling near — too near — to the naked flame . . .

Immediately, in one sickening second, there was a flare of flame, cries of alarm. Instinctively, Sally reacted. Reaching into the carrycot, she snatched up a baby blanket and threw it over the screaming child.

It was all over in a couple of seconds — the flame extinguished, the child unhurt; more put out by the damage to her fancy-dress costume than anything else!

"Oh God — thank you, Sister! I might have killed her." With a look of pure horror on his face, the young father put away his lighter, and the colour gradually came back to his shocked face.

The little girl was soon comforted, and by the time the coming of Santa's sleigh was announced, she had completely forgotten the incident. As Sally stood watching a well-padded Dai Jones give each child its special toy, saying just the right thing, bringing joy and happiness to all the kiddies there, she looked round for Richard. Huw, she knew, would be in later after his evening surgery.

As her eyes scanned the crowded room, she felt a light touch on her arm from behind.

"Looking for me, *cariad*?" and her heart leapt to the sound of that well-beloved voice. And because he spoke the truth, she turned a flushed, embarrassed face to deny it!

"Apart from the little skirmish just now — are you having a good time, Sally?" So he had seen that near accident?

"Great! Don't forget it's the first works' party I've ever been to . . . "

"M'm, and may I say you grace it beautifully, darling? Will you come with me for a moment — I've something to give you — in my office, it's quieter there." There was a touch of uncertainty in his manner, but Sally followed him obediently, saying,

"A present? I've got something for you, Richard, at home. I'll bring it . . . "

He switched on the small desk light,

and closing the door firmly, turned to face her.

"It's this first, Sally . . . " And with a rather sheepish look on his face, he produced a small sprig of mistletoe.

"Oh Richard — what a corny old gag . . . " Sally's laughing mouth was suddenly covered by his, firmly shutting off any further words.

"Darling Sally, you drive me crazy, did you know that? Especially in that frock," he dropped a kiss on her bare shoulder. "I've been longing to tell you how much I love you, but . . . "

In a daze, Sally pushed against his chest.

"Love me? But you've always been so — so awful to me. Right from that very first interview, you've seemed to despise me."

Holding her loosely round her slim waist, he nodded and then leaned back to go on —

"I know — it was because of Philip!"

She gasped, her eyes wide with shock.

"Philip! How did you — who told you . . . ?" The words tumbled from trembling lips as light suddenly dawned.

"Let's sit down, Sally — here . . . "
and he pulled her down on to his lap as
he sat in the big swivel chair.

"Oh yes, I know about Philip!" His
voice was cold with scorn then. "I should
do — he's married to my sister!"

"No — no!" White-faced, her eyes
dark with dismay, Sally looked into his
face and saw only the truth there.

"Oh yes," he replied. "She knows he
plays around. More fool her, but he
always comes back to her. Of course,
she holds the purse strings," he added
bitterly.

Seeing the puzzlement on her face at
that, he went on,

"No, we're not a wealthy family, but
my sister is! Her god-mother went out
to Australia with her husband, and they
made a fortune; left it all to her lucky god-
daughter, and that's why Philip married
her in the first place, I reckon."

And Sally, remembering the rather
plain girl he'd said was his sister, saw
it all too clearly.

"I didn't know when I put your
application on the short list — not
then. But just before the interview, I

had occasion to ring up Matron at Saint Christine's to check your references. She was busy for a minute or two, so I held on . . . and was duly entertained by her secretary . . . "

"Mavis!" Sally gasped.

"Yes, the bitchy Mavis, who lost no time in putting me in the picture! Of how you were forced to leave because you'd been found out — how you'd chased Philip, a married doctor! Of course, she didn't know he was my brother-in-law," he paused and then went on, "Not quite the coincidence it seems — I knew Saint Christine's was a good teaching hospital. It was a point in your favour on the way to the short list."

As he stopped for breath, the thoughts were racing around in Sally's head.

"So by the time I came for the interview . . . ?" He nodded.

"That's right. The only thing is, Sally my love, I began to fancy you like mad, from that very first day. God knows I've been fighting it ever since, until . . . "

Sally waited, her heart heavy. He hadn't ever trusted her, had he? Real love brings complete trust, so how could

254

he say he loved her?

"When you started to go around with Huw, I wondered who to believe — Mavis and the facts — or my own heart."

"So — why the change?" There was a remoteness in Sally's voice, and the eyes he turned to her then were filled with remorse and a sort of anguish.

"Huw came into my office yesterday. Told me that when you refused his offer of marriage, you told him that there had never been anything — er — really between you and Philip. He believed you. 'No more than kissing and petting,' he said."

"I suppose if I'd have told you that you wouldn't have believed me?" she burst out bitterly. He gave a deep sigh of penitent regret.

"Sally, my dearest, it's been such a muddle. You didn't know I was Philip's brother-in-law, and that I'd been trying hard to despise you. But I failed miserably, *cariad*. I *do* love you; have done so for a long time now. Huw suggested — hinted that he thought you sort of liked me a bit." He broke off, his dark eyes pleading for her understanding.

"You needed *his* confirmation though, didn't you?" she accused miserably. Dear heavens, how she longed to believe him!

"Not really, sweetheart. You see I'd already bought this. I was going to ask you — beg you — to love me in return."

Without moving her off his lap, he reached into a pocket and drew out a small black velvet-covered box and opened it. In it was a gorgeous engagement ring, its diamonds gleaming brilliantly in the dim light.

"I bought this the weekend you went home, Sally. I — I missed you so much. Please let me put it on — my Christmas present to you — with all my love?"

Sally nodded, too full to speak, and her eyes filled with tears of happiness as she watched him slide the beautiful ring on to her finger.

"It fits . . . " she breathed.

"I know. Megan helped me out there . . . "

But his words didn't register; she reached out to coil slender arms round his neck.

"Oh Richard, I do love you. I'll die if

you ever stop wanting me."

It took a long time to finally convince her that she need have no fears on that score!

"And to think that all I got you was an antique brass trivet for the fireplace in your cottage," she giggled.

"Our cottage . . . ?" Dark eyebrows rose, a long finger tracing a loving pattern down her soft cheek.

"Yes, please, Richard."

Firmly then, he set her upon her feet.

"Good, that's settled. Now let's go and tell everybody the good news . . . "

A real PO to the last, Sally thought in a happy daze.

THE WILDERNESS WALK
Sheila Bishop

Stifling unpleasant memories of a misbegotten romance in Cleave with Lord Francis Aubrey, Lavinia goes on holiday there with her sister. The two women are thrust into a romantic intrigue involving none other than Lord Francis.

THE RELUCTANT GUEST
Rosalind Brett

Ann Calvert went to spend a month on a South African farm with Theo Borland and his sister. They both proved to be different from her first idea of them, and there was Storr Peterson — the most disturbing man she had ever met.

ONE ENCHANTED SUMMER
Anne Tedlock Brooks

A tale of mystery and romance and a girl who found both during one enchanted summer.

CLOUD OVER MALVERTON
Nancy Buckingham

Dulcie soon realises that something is seriously wrong at Malverton, and when violence strikes she is horrified to find herself under suspicion of murder.

AFTER THOUGHTS
Max Bygraves

The Cockney entertainer tells stories of his East End childhood, of his RAF days, and his post-war showbusiness successes and friendships with fellow comedians.

MOONLIGHT AND MARCH ROSES
D. Y. Cameron

Lynn's search to trace a missing girl takes her to Spain, where she meets Clive Hendon. While untangling the situation, she untangles her emotions and decides on her own future.

NURSE ALICE IN LOVE
Theresa Charles

Accepting the post of nurse to little Fernie Sherrod, Alice Everton could not guess at the romance, suspense and danger which lay ahead at the Sherrod's isolated estate.

POIROT INVESTIGATES
Agatha Christie

Two things bind these eleven stories together — the brilliance and uncanny skill of the diminutive Belgian detective, and the stupidity of his Watson-like partner, Captain Hastings.

LET LOOSE THE TIGERS
Josephine Cox

Queenie promised to find the long-lost son of the frail, elderly murderess, Hannah Jason. But her enquiries threatened to unlock the cage where crucial secrets had long been held captive.

THE TWILIGHT MAN
Frank Gruber

Jim Rand lives alone in the California desert awaiting death. Into his hermit existence comes a teenage girl who blows both his past and his brief future wide open.

DOG IN THE DARK
Gerald Hammond

Jim Cunningham breeds and trains gun dogs, and his antagonism towards the devotees of show spaniels earns him many enemies. So when one of them is found murdered, the police are on his doorstep within hours.

THE RED KNIGHT
Geoffrey Moxon

When he finds himself a pawn on the chessboard of international espionage with his family in constant danger, Guy Trent becomes embroiled in moves and countermoves which may mean life or death for Western scientists.

TIGER TIGER
Frank Ryan

A young man involved in drugs is found murdered. This is the first event which will draw Detective Inspector Sandy Woodings into a whirlpool of murder and deceit.

CAROLINE MINUSCULE
Andrew Taylor

Caroline Minuscule, a medieval script, is the first clue to the whereabouts of a cache of diamonds. The search becomes a deadly kind of fairy story in which several murders have an other-worldly quality.

LONG CHAIN OF DEATH
Sarah Wolf

During the Second World War four American teenagers from the same town join the Army together. Forty-two years later, the son of one of the soldiers realises that someone is systematically wiping out the families of the four men.

THE LISTERDALE MYSTERY
Agatha Christie

Twelve short stories ranging from the light-hearted to the macabre, diverse mysteries ingeniously and plausibly contrived and convincingly unravelled.

TO BE LOVED
Lynne Collins

Andrew married the woman he had always loved despite the knowledge that Sarah married him for reasons of her own. So much heartache could have been avoided if only he had known how vital it was to be loved.

ACCUSED NURSE
Jane Converse

Paula found herself accused of a crime which could cost her her job, her nurse's reputation, and even the man she loved, unless the truth came to light.

BUTTERFLY MONTANE
Dorothy Cork

Parma had come to New Guinea to marry Alec Rivers, but she found him completely disinterested and that overbearing Pierce Adams getting entirely the wrong idea about her.

HONOURABLE FRIENDS
Janet Daley

Priscilla Burford is happily married when she meets Junior Environment Minister Alistair Thurston. Inevitably, sexual obsession and political necessity collide.

WANDERING MINSTRELS
Mary Delorme

Stella Wade's career as a concert pianist might have been ruined by the rudeness of a famous conductor, so it seemed to her agent and benefactor. Even Sir Nicholas fails to see the possibilities when John Tallis falls deeply in love with Stella.

MORNING IS BREAKING
Lesley Denny

The growing frenzy of war catapults Diane Clements into a clandestine marriage and separation with a German refugee.

LAST BUS TO WOODSTOCK
Colin Dexter

A girl's body is discovered huddled in the courtyard of a Woodstock pub, and Detective Chief Inspector Morse and Sergeant Lewis are hunting a rapist and a murderer.

THE STUBBORN TIDE
Anne Durham

Everyone advised Carol not to grieve so excessively over her cousin's death. She might have followed their advice if the man she loved thought that way about her, but another girl came first in his affections.